Milo March is a hard-drin[...] James-Bondian character. He [...] combination of personality, blu..., bravado, luck, skill, experience, and intellect. He is a shrewd judge of human character, a crack shot, and a deeper character than I have found in most of the other spy/thriller novels I've read. But, above all, he is a con-man—and a very good one. It is Milo March himself who makes the series worth reading.

—Don Miller, *The Mystery Nook* fanzine 12

Steeger Books is proud to reissue twenty-three vintage novels and stories by M.E. Chaber, whose Milo March Mysteries deliver mile-a-minute action and breezily readable entertainment for thriller buffs.

Milo is an Insurance Investigator who takes on the tough cases. Organized crime, grand theft, arson, suspicious disappearances, murders, and millions and millions of dollars—whatever it is, Milo is just the man for the job. Or even the only man for it.

During World War II, Milo was assigned to the OSS and later the CIA. Now in the Army Reserves, with the rank of Major, he is recalled for special jobs behind the Iron Curtain. As an agent, he chops necks, trusses men like chickens to steal their uniforms, shoots point blank at secret police—yet shows compassion to an agent from the other side.

Whatever Milo does, he knows how to do it right. When the work is completed, he returns to his favorite things: women, booze, and good food, more or less in that order....

THE MILO MARCH MYSTERIES

Hangman's Harvest
No Grave for March
The Man Inside
As Old as Cain
The Splintered Man
A Lonely Walk
The Gallows Garden
A Hearse of Another Color
So Dead the Rose
Jade for a Lady
Softly in the Night
Uneasy Lies the Dead
Six Who Ran
Wanted: Dead Men
The Day It Rained Diamonds
A Man in the Middle
Wild Midnight Falls
The Flaming Man
Green Grow the Graves
The Bonded Dead
Born to Be Hanged
Death to the Brides
The Twisted Trap: Six Milo March Stories

The Splintered Man

KENDELL FOSTER CROSSEN
Writing as
M.E. CHABER

With an Afterword by
KENDRA CROSSEN BURROUGHS

STEEGER BOOKS / **2020**

PUBLISHED BY STEEGER BOOKS
Visit steegerbooks.com for more books like this.

PUBLISHING HISTORY

Hardcover
New York: Rinehart & Co., October 1955.
Toronto: Clarke, Irwin & Company, November 1955.
London: T. V. Boardman (American Bloodhound Espionage Mystery #145), 1957. Dust jacket by Denis McLoughlin.

Paperback
New York: Mystery Guild, March 1956.
New York: Permabook #M-3080, April 1957. Cover by Robert E. Schulz.
New York: Paperback Library (63-306), A Milo March Mystery, #7, April 1970. Cover by Robert McGinnis.

ISBN: 978-1-61827-507-3

Vivamus, mea Martha, atque amemus …

CONTENTS

Two drugs are mentioned prominently in this novel. Everything said about lysergic acid diethylamide (LSD) is as accurate as I could make it. I have taken certain liberties with chlorpromazine in extrapolating the uses to which it may still be put. As for the rest, while actual events and the names of actual organizations and persons are generously sprinkled through the novel—we live in an age where reality borrows heavily from fiction, and fiction must return the compliment in order to survive—it is purely a product of the author's imagination. None of the characters is meant to portray any person living or dead. Aside from that, any similarity to the world about us is entirely intentional.

M.E.C.

ONE

Ten years is a long time. That was how long it had been since I took off my uniform, put on a civilian suit, and, with my discharge papers making a warm spot in my pocket, went out to buy the loudest tie I could find. The war was over. They were never going to catch me playing footsie with the Army again.

I was still a reserve officer. For a while that worried me, but the years rolled by and nothing happened. I kept busy as an insurance investigator, working out of Denver, Colorado. I galloped past the middle thirties, getting a couple of inches thicker in the middle, and began to feel that the Defense Department was no longer breathing down the back of my neck. I got married and acquired a son the same day—by adoption.* I felt I was beginning to make quite a career out of being a civilian.

That was when they hit me. It was a day that started out like any other day. I got up fairly late and looked at the mail while I had my breakfast. In the middle of it, my coffee turned to wormwood. There was a little note that said I was to report the following day, in uniform, for active duty.

---

* Milo meets Greta Brooks in East Berlin in *No Grave for March* and marries her in America in *As Old as Cain*. Ernesto, the boy they adopt in order to legitimize his illegal entry into the U.S., appears in *The Man Inside* and *As Old as Cain*. (All footnotes were added by the editor.)

My breakfast was ruined, so I went down to the office. First I tried to find out why the Army once more had designs on me. I talked to some bright young lieutenant who knew from nothing. Next I tried to pull my few little strings. I made a call to a general I knew in Washington. He wasn't in, or, at least, that's what the efficient WAC said. I suspected that she had to ask him first. That should have tipped me off, but it didn't.

I went in to see the man I worked for. His name was Niels Bancroft and he didn't value a dollar any more than his jugular vein. But he had one weak spot. He believed that people—other people—should jump at the chance to work for the government. He had once loaned me to the State Department. The fact that I was being recalled by the Army brightened up his entire day. He told me to take the rest of the day off to buy my uniform and assured me my job would be waiting even if I didn't get out for another fifteen years. The cheerful approach.

Working out careful plans for a personal vendetta, I bought a uniform. One, going on the forlorn premise that the Army would realize they'd made a mistake. Then I went home and sulked. The next morning I disguised myself as an officer and a gentleman and went downtown. I was sworn in by a vacant-eyed colonel, who wasn't any brighter than the lieutenant. Then I was given my orders. I was to proceed immediately by plane to Washington, D.C. That was all.

"What the hell do I do when I get to the Washington airfield?" I asked. "Just hang around the coffee shop until the Chief of Staff drops in for a cup of coffee?"

"I really couldn't say," the colonel said. He was staring

somewhere over my left shoulder. "I imagine you'll receive new orders upon landing. Have a nice flight, Major."

"Thanks," I said dryly.

I went out to the Denver airport and got on a plane. It was getting dark when we landed in Washington. As I came off the plane I heard my name on the loudspeaker. I was wanted at the information counter.

A very pretty WAC sergeant was waiting there. Blonde and stacked. Even the military couldn't figure out a way to cut a uniform to hide her curves. If she'd been a French model, Christian Dior would've had a nervous breakdown.

When I'd identified myself, she saluted and handed me an envelope. Sealed orders, just like in the movies. I ripped it open and looked at the single sheet of paper. It gave an address and an office number. I was to report there at twenty hundred. I looked at my watch. I had about fifteen minutes.

"They must be afraid I'll wander around and be picked by a recruiting officer," I said. "Or that I'll buy a sandwich and stick it on an expense account."

The WAC stared at me, big-eyed, and I realized I wasn't showing the old team spirit.

I read the address aloud. "Where is it?"

"About ten minutes away, sir," she said.

"Okay," I said. "I'll get a cab and go over."

"I have a car outside, sir. My orders are to drive you to your destination."

I looked her over again. "The Army's improving in one respect," I said. "The escort service is better, but they don't allow enough time to take advantage of it. I must speak to the General about it."

She turned without answering and led the way out of the terminal. I followed, enjoying the view. She was probably wearing a Government Issue girdle, but the movement was strictly her own. That was one maneuver the Articles of War had forgotten to take into consideration.

There was an Army car in front of the terminal. We climbed in and she started the motor.

"What is this place?" I asked.

"I don't know, sir." She slipped the car expertly into the stream of traffic.

"That's what I like about the Army," I said, lighting a cigarette. "Nobody ever knows anything. Well, I don't suppose they'll put me on a night shift. How about hanging around until I've reported in and then you can show me around? I'm ten years behind on latrine gossip."

She looked as shocked as if I'd suggested raping her in the lobby of the Pentagon. "I couldn't, sir," she said. "My orders are to report back to my superior as soon as I've delivered you to your destination."

"At ease, Sergeant," I said, grinning. "Stop quivering your stripes at me."

She laughed and continued to concentrate on her driving.

The address turned out to be an ordinary office building. I got out of the car, took a last look at the sergeant's military profile, and went in. The office number I wanted was 321. I took the elevator to the third floor. A moment later I was reading my orders over for the third time and wondering who was crazy. There was no 321.

I wandered up and down the corridors several times. Most of the offices were dark. And there was no 321. Finally I decided that somebody had goofed and to hell with it. I headed back for the elevators.

There was a young man standing in front of them. He watched me come down the corridor.

"Looking for something, Major?" he asked.

"Yeah," I grunted. "Three twenty-one."

He shook his head. "No such number on this floor. Who're you looking for?"

It was a casual question. Too casual. I took a closer look at him. Everything about him was just a little too casual. I began to get annoyed.

"I came to Washington to improve my golf game," I said. "I need a few lessons on my chip shots, only I don't have a chippy. I thought maybe I'd find one here."

I was right. His face got a little red. West Point cholera. They all get it when they're not in a position to pull rank.

"I was just trying to be helpful," he said. He was still trying to sound like an aggrieved citizen, but it was counterfeit.

"Sure," I said. "But you're a bird dog. I can smell them. They've all got that doggy smell—if you know what I mean."

He knew what I meant. His face got a darker red. "You're to go to room three sixteen," he said stiffly.

I lit a cigarette and tossed the match at his feet. "I don't like games. Maybe I'll just go back and wait until the Army decides to act grown up."

"You're under orders."

"Issued by an idiot," I said. I swung around and went back down the corridor.

Three sixteen was across the hall from where I'd been looking. There was a light behind the frosted glass. I opened the door and went in. I was in a reception room, but there was nobody there to receive me. There was another door on the other side of the room. I heard the murmur of voices from behind it. I went across and threw the door open.

There were three men sitting there, facing the doorway where I stood. Two of them were civilians, looking prosperous and bureaucratic. The third was an Army officer. With three stars on his shoulders. I didn't know the civilians, but I knew the General. His name was Sam Roberts. Back in World War II, he and I had been in the OSS together. He'd been a colonel then. Some eight years later I'd done a job for the State Department and Sam Roberts had been in on that.* By then he was wearing two stars. Now he'd added a third. He was a busy man.

The General was in G-2. That meant that he was probably responsible for my recall to active service and for the little game of the wrong office number and the G-2 bird dog who'd tried to pump me.

There was a movement back of me. I glanced around. It was the bird dog. He was still annoyed, but no more than I was.

"He caught on at once, sir," the bird dog reported. "I would say he rates high on performance and low on attitude, sir."

"That sounds familiar," General Roberts grunted. "That's all, Rand." He waited until the bird dog drifted away, then

---

* See *No Grave for March* by M.E. Chaber.

turned his gaze on me. His voice took on a parade-ground bark. "Your name?"

"Milo March," I snapped. "I knew you were senile, but I didn't know it had progressed so far as to forget names."

I saw a muscle in his jaw twitching the way it always did when he was on the point of threatening me with court-martial.

"Your rank?" he demanded.

"Apprentice Boy Scout," I said. "These bronze oak leaves on my shoulders merely mean that I belong to the Forest Patrol."

The two civilians were hiding grins behind their hands. General Roberts was struggling with himself. I could see the wheels clicking as he tried to decide whether to sacrifice me or some of the shine on the three stars. Finally he decided to treat the whole thing as a joke—just between us boys.

He gave West Point's version of a hearty grin and turned to the two civilians. "March always was an insubordinate son of a bitch," he said. "When we were in the OSS together, I used to threaten to court-martial him every other day. But I must admit that when it came to delivering the goods, he was the best man I ever worked with. That's why I said he's the only man for our present job."

"Let me get this straight," I said. "Are you the joker who had me recalled to active service?"

He nodded.

"And it was your idea to give me the wrong office number and then post some dumb staff officer, disguised as a human, to see if I'd shoot off my mouth?"

He nodded again. "This is a delicate operation, and I had to be sure you were on your toes. Civilian life softens up a lot of men."

"Not as much as the Army softens up some heads," I said. I went on to give him my most intimate thoughts about the Army and more specifically about a three-star general named Sam Roberts. I didn't stop until I'd run out of breath.

"We can understand how you feel about being recalled, Major March," one of the civilians said smoothly, "but I think I can assure you that it won't be for long. We have one assignment for you and, as soon as that's finished, you'll be out of uniform again."

"Who are these jokers?" I asked the General.

"Mr. George Hillyer, the head of the Central Intelligence Agency, and his assistant, Mr. Philip Emerson."

"You in the CIA, too?"

"No," Roberts said, "but as head of G-2, I work very closely with Mr. Hillyer on many problems. In this particular case, you've been recalled and assigned to work with the CIA."

"Under whose orders?"

"Mr. Hillyer's, of course."

"Good," I said, grinning. "If I had to work under you, I might as well cut my throat now and save the wear and tear on my nerves."

That pinked him right in the West Point equivalent of his heart. "Don't forget I can still court-martial you."

"You ever try it," I said, "and I'll tell the court how you became a colonel. Remember the night you were delirious in a ditch in Yugoslavia and told me all the details?"

His face got a dark red and he looked as if he were about to flip a star.

"Gentlemen," George Hillyer put in before the General could get under way, "I appreciate the fact that this is in the nature of a reunion for both of you, but I think we'd better get down to cases. Major March, I understand that two years ago you went into East Berlin for the State Department. Do you think you could do it again?"

"Sure," I said. "It's easy to go to East Berlin. All you do is get on the subway in West Berlin and get off at the first station after the Potsdamer Platz. You can get out by reversing the process."*

"It won't be quite that simple in this case," he said dryly. "We also want you to find a man and bring him out. We're not even sure that he's still in East Berlin. He was there a week ago. By now, he may be anywhere in East Germany—or even in Russia. We want you to find him wherever he is and bring him out. We know it's a tall order."

"March can do it if anyone can," General Roberts growled. He glared at me. "And that's the only reason he isn't under arrest right this minute."

I ignored him. "Who's the lucky man?"

"Hermann Gruss."

I whistled. I recognized the name all right. It had been

* At the time of this story, the Berlin Wall dividing the city into East and West Berlin had not yet been built, which is why the Soviet sector is just a subway ride away. One of the reasons for the closing of the border, enforced by the building of the Wall, was the emigration or "brain drain" of scientists and others whose intellectual skills were needed by the Communists. This fact accounts for the concern over defection and kidnapping that also informs the plot of *No Grave for March*. The border was closed by East Germany in August 1961. It was finally reopened in 1989, and the Wall was demolished by 1990.

appearing in all the newspapers for the last three weeks. Hermann Gruss had been, up until then, the head of the counterespionage police in West Germany. Before that he'd been a famous anti-Nazi, one of the few to escape after the unsuccessful bomb plot against Hitler. Now he'd gone over to the Communists in the East.

"Wherever he is," I said, "they'll probably have the whole Soviet army guarding him."

"Probably," Hillyer admitted calmly. "But we've got to find some way of getting him away from them. Hermann Gruss is worth almost an entire army to the Reds. Think you can pull it off?"

I shrugged. "How the hell do I know? I can try. But isn't it a little like shutting the barn door after the horse is stolen? By this time he must have already done his damage."

"He's done plenty," Hillyer admitted. "A hundred Western agents have been picked up in East Germany since Gruss went behind the Curtain. But that's only a fraction of the damage Gruss can do. He didn't have any list of Western agents, except his own, but he possesses enough information to ferret them out slowly. In addition to that, he has too much information about our methods; it makes it possible for him to interpret almost our every move."

"No wonder," grunted General Roberts. There was considerable malice in his voice. "He got the grand, conducted tour of the Central Intelligence Agency."

Hillyer looked uncomfortable. "Unfortunately, that's true. As part of our program of working closely with the West German government, Gruss was brought over here recently and instructed in our latest counterespionage techniques. This necessitated revealing a great many of our methods. It couldn't be helped."

"He got nothing from the Army," the General said smugly.

"Who has?" I murmured, winning another glare from the General. "You're sure that Gruss has sold out to the Reds?"

"No, we're not sure," Hillyer said. "Oh, he's helping them, all right, but we're not sure that he's doing it voluntarily."

"Speak for yourself, Hillyer," General Roberts snorted. "Of course, he's doing it voluntarily. In fact, G-2 has known for some time that Gruss was a double agent. He's always played both sides. Even when he was supposed to be such a great anti-Nazi, he was a spy for Hitler. That's why the bomb plot against Hitler failed in 1944."

"Good heavens, General," Hillyer said, "the man's own father and sister were executed for taking part in that plot, and Gruss himself escaped only by a matter of seconds."

"Since when have the Nazis and Communists objected to sending their families to be executed?" the General demanded.

Hillyer's face smoothed out and he turned back to me. "This is, more or less, a family quarrel. There are still many theories about Gruss's going behind the Curtain. Some believe he was a double agent. A few think that Gruss is a perfectly sincere man who became convinced that the Nazis were again getting control in West Germany and that only in the East would he get help in fighting them. Still others believe that either black-mail or illness is at the bottom of it."

"Which do you favor?" I asked.

"We haven't reached a definite conclusion yet," Hillyer said slowly. "We do think, however, that Dr. Franz Oderbruch plays an important role in the answer. Incidentally, if you could manage to bring back both Oderbruch and Gruss, we'd be most grateful."

"Dr. Oderbruch?" I asked. The name was familiar, but I couldn't place it. I hadn't followed the news stories too closely.

He nodded. "Dr. Franz Oderbruch. He was a West Berlin physician. He was a fairly active anti-Nazi and was presumed to be an anti-Communist although he was not active. In recent years, he has seemed to be more a playboy than anything else. He and Gruss were friendly, and he had been treating Gruss."

"For what?"

"Originally, my opinion was that Gruss was merely a hypochondriac. When he was here, he complained of being ill and on a few days didn't show up at all. But he refused to see any of our doctors, relying on pills that Dr. Oderbruch had given him. Since the disappearance of both men, there has been a theory that Gruss had cancer and Oderbruch convinced him that he could only be helped in East Berlin. We have had one report that Gruss is at a hospital in the Eastern sector. Dr. Oderbruch is on the staff of that hospital, having a practice in both sectors."

"Oderbruch went with Gruss?" I asked.

"Yes. They went to the East in Oderbruch's car. They crossed at an East-West sector checkpoint at about midnight. At three o'clock in the morning, Dr. Oderbruch returned to his apartment in West Berlin and took all of his personal papers from his safe, then went back to the East sector. That's the last we've heard of the doctor."

General Roberts snorted, but didn't say anything.

"You have a plan on this or do I play it by ear?" I asked.

"We're leaving it up to you," Hillyer said. "General Roberts has told us you'd prefer it that way. We've prepared a set of forged papers for you to use in East Berlin. We can also supply you with a place to live there—in a rooming house run by a woman who is a Western agent. In addition, we will give you the name of one other agent you can call upon for help. The rest is up to you."

"Good," I said. "You have a dossier on Gruss?"

"We have one, but we're going to let you compile your own on the spot. You may pick up a lot that's missing from our report, since the investigation is still going on. Incidentally, Major, that was one of the reasons for having you recalled to uniform. You'll be less conspicuous while investigating, since there'll be a lot of servicemen doing the same thing."

"Oh, my God," I said. "You mean there'll be a lot of military mental midgets mucking around?"

Hillyer smiled. "That's only part of it, I'm afraid. In addition to Army, Navy, and Air Intelligence, there'll be State Department men and a couple of our agents. Then there will be investigators from the West German Police, any number of men from British and French Intelligence, plus quite a few amateurs, I expect."

"Amateurs?"

"Yes. The West German government has offered an award of six hundred thousand deutsche marks—that's close to a hundred and fifty thousand dollars—for information that will fully explain why Gruss suddenly defected."

I groaned. "If there ever was a clue, it'll be trampled beyond recognition by the time I get there."

"I'm sure of it," he agreed, "but at least you'll probably be able to get a good picture of Gruss and Oderbruch, and that may help even more than a so-called clue. When you think you've got enough, you can shed the uniform and go over. In the meantime, one of our men in West Berlin will give you the leads they have and go around with you if you like."

"When do I leave?" I asked.

Hillyer glanced at the General. "In the morning," he said. "We're flying a couple of replacement officers into Berlin and you'll go along."

"Okay," I said. "But I want to get one thing straight before I take off."

"What's that?"

"The minute the job's finished, I get out of the Army." I wanted to get it all clear. I'd been pretty rough with the General, and I knew he had a memory as long as his service record.

"As soon as we can process you out," he said.

"No dice," I said flatly. "I want your word, as an officer—and a gentleman by act of Congress—that I'll be out the same day that I land back in the States. I don't trust the weight of those three stars on your shoulders. It's going to be the way I say or you can start court-martialing me right now."

He was angry, but he was still more interested in getting the job done than in pulling rank. "All right, Milo," he said.

"I give you my word that you'll be discharged the day you reach Washington."

"And no hanky-panky about military orders that will keep me away from Washington?"

He laughed reluctantly and glanced at Hillyer. "You know," he said, "it's a good thing that March has always been successful; otherwise he would have been qualifying for the longest residence in Leavenworth." He swung back to face me. "I will give orders that as soon as you return to West Germany from your mission, you are to be flown immediately to Washington and discharged upon your arrival. Satisfactory, Major?"

"Satisfactory, General," I said. I gave him a salute with the thumb of my hand closer to my nose than regulations called for. It was the way I used to salute him when he gave me orders back of the lines in the late war.

I could see him remembering. He leaned back in his chair and sighed heavily. "It was a great war," he said.

It was one of his favorite remarks. That will give you a rough idea why I didn't trust him any more than I did.

TWO

It was two years since I'd been in Berlin, but I could see a difference even as an Army car drove me into the heart of the city. There had been a lot of rebuilding so that the scars of war were disappearing. There was a difference, also, in the attitudes of the people I saw on the street. They walked with more of the old German arrogance, and I found myself wondering how long it would be before they'd be goose-stepping again.

My first stop was at Army headquarters, where I reported to a Colonel Fred Phillips of G-2. He was a bright young man who wore his silver eagles with an arrogance not too different from what I'd just been seeing on the streets of Berlin. He didn't show any great enthusiasm for another officer fresh from the States.

"What the hell's wrong with the Pentagon?" he demanded, speaking more to himself than to me. He obviously knew nothing about my mission except that I was after information about Gruss. "We've covered every angle on Gruss. I've got plenty of men on it and they're all familiar with Berlin and with the situation. How the hell do they expect a new man to contribute anything?"

"You know how it is in the Army," I told him. "The General believes that many hands confuse the issue."

He didn't care for my attitude. The starch that West Point

had poured in his spine began to harden. "I'm sure General Roberts knows what he's doing," he said coldly. "My only question is I don't know what the hell you can do for us."

"I wasn't expecting to do anything for you," I said. "My orders are to make an independent investigation."

"I know." That was what was bothering him. He didn't like anyone being independent of his command. He stared at me coldly. "I don't seem to remember your name, Major. Where were you stationed before?"

"In a tweed suit," I said. "I was recalled to active duty yesterday."

"Oh, my God," he said, summing up his opinion of civilians. Then he pulled himself together, determined to carry on despite the usual obstacles. The Articles of War crept back into his voice. "My orders, Major March, are to make our files available to you. What would you like to know?"

"Nothing." I grinned at the surprise on his face. I had made up my mind to depend on the CIA files rather than the Army's. G-2's theory about Gruss might be right, but the fact that they were so sure of themselves might blind them to a lot of things that would help me.

"Then what are you doing here?"

"Reporting to a superior officer, sir."

"All right," he said. He shook his head. "I'll admit, Major, that I don't like this, but my orders don't seem to leave me any choice." Having summed up the situation, he handled it in a typical military fashion. He shuffled the papers on his desk and looked at me coldly. "In the meantime, I'm pretty busy, Major."

I took the hint. I gave him a snappy salute, swung around, and marched out. I found David Farley, the CIA man, in offices only a block away, but in general attitude he and Colonel Phillips were more than a block apart. Farley was about forty and there was a quiet air of competence about him. Although he had a certain wariness—not surprising in anyone who had ridden through the Congressional investigations—he was friendly and cooperative.

There was another man with him when I was shown into his office. He was young, probably still under thirty, but he had the wise, careful look you see on so many of the young men in Washington.

"Glad to see you, Major March," Farley said after he had identified himself. "This is Martin Lane, our security officer here."

"Hi, Major," Lane said. His voice was friendly but impersonal. That was understandable. When a man spends all his time setting others up for the ax because of their activities or friends, he probably soon decides it's wiser not to have friends at all.

"You're wasting your time having him here," I told Farley. "I can tell you that I'm not a good security risk. I don't live that carefully."

The security officer laughed heartily, but there was a false note in it. "I'll say you don't," he said. "If nothing else, we could pin your Party membership back on you." He was referring to the fact that when I'd done a job for the State Department two years before, I'd gotten into East Berlin in the guise of an American Communist.

"It wouldn't surprise me a bit," I told him seriously. "If the Senator ever ran across it, he'd certainly start polishing his own apples with it."

"You don't have to worry about that," Farley said quickly. Too quickly. "Martin, here, is a very good friend of the Senator's." So that was it. He was warning me.

"Oh," I said. I managed to pack a lot of my feeling into that brief grunt.

Martin Lane's smile had gotten a little tighter. "I'm sure the Major knows that I was joking," he said. He looked at me. "I'll probably be seeing you around, Major, before you go over to visit our friends." He gave me a casual wave of his hand and walked out.

I glanced at Farley. "He knows why I'm here?"

"He and I are the only ones who know about it. Not that the 'only' means much. Our people are pretty good at guessing things, and there are always a few inner leaks that sometimes become outer leaks." He stared blankly at the papers on his desk. "Martin's a good security officer, and you don't have to worry about him being in on the secret. It might be well, however, to remember that he does have many friends back in Washington."

I grinned at him. "You mean that you've heard I have a big mouth and that I'd better keep my political opinions to myself?"

He looked up and grinned back at me. "My coded message from Hillyer mentioned that you were a man of strong opinions." He leaned back in his chair. "A hell of a way to make a living, isn't it?"

"Don't give it a thought," I said. "You're a hero, my boy. You can look forward either to getting a pension or having your scalp dangling from the sport belt of some politician."

"I think about it sometimes, but I'm too old to learn another trade," he said. He lit a cigarette. "But, seriously, I had to let Martin in on your reason for being here. He knows all of our personnel better than I do, and I had to pick out someone to help you."

"I don't need any special help," I said. "I know Berlin."

"You'll need help. Since the government offered a reward for information about Gruss, there're a couple thousand amateur detectives nosing around. Without help, you won't be able to get near any of the people who can give you information."

"Okay."

"We've got two men who can help you. Willi Borm is on very friendly terms with both Ursula Hamack, Oderbruch's nurse, and Freda Gruss. Both women have had to go into hiding from the amateurs."

"Who's Freda Gruss?"

"His wife." He saw the surprise on my face. "Yeah, he left her behind. That's one of the reasons we don't fully accept the Army theory that he was a double agent. However, we're keeping an eye on her in case he sends for her."

"Willi Borm a German?"

He nodded. "He's been working for us the last couple of years. A very reliable man. The other man who will help you is a French employee of ours. Henri Flambeau. He can steer you around to some of the spots where you can meet some of the shadier characters who knew Gruss and Oderbruch. Both of them have been instructed to be at your disposal. One day with Willi and a couple of evenings with Henri should do the job. Then you'll be ready to go over."

"Fine."

"In the meantime," he said, "you can go through our files on Gruss, or I'll be glad to answer any questions you want to ask. After that, I'm afraid, you'll have to go on your own. We're practically on around-the-clock shifts just now."

"Something new?"

"Yeah—at least partly new. We've been having a lot of night raids by gangs of young Communists from the East. There have been two kinds of operations. They've been breaking into offices and taking harmless invoices or other papers. They've also been breaking into factories and military installations and leaving empty metal boxes."

"That doesn't make much sense."

"It does and it doesn't," he said. "We've figured out part of it. All of the gangs are students in an espionage school the Russians are running in East Germany. We know that Carinhall—the estate that once belonged to Goering—is being used as such a school. The raids are, we're sure, part of their training. They send them after harmless papers, until they learn the art, so that if they're caught the offense won't be so severe."

"What about the metal boxes that are empty?"

He looked at me soberly. "They are about the size and weight of small atom bombs."

I whistled softly.

"We're still trying to crack a number of problems about it," he said, "but there's one angle we especially want to break. Every one of these gangs has been absolutely fearless. Not the usual fanatic thing we expect, but something different."

"Drugs?" I guessed.

"That's why we're so interested. Two weeks ago, one of the raiders was killed by a watchman. We had an autopsy performed on him. There was no evidence of any known drug." He made an elaborate ceremony of putting out his cigarette before glancing up at me. "The reason I mention this is that Dr. Oderbruch took over the office and the practice of an important Nazi doctor—who had been experimenting with drugs. That's why we're as interested in getting Dr. Oderbruch back as we are in getting Gruss. Think you could manage it?"

"I can try."

"Good," he said. "We can't ask any more than that. Now, what would you like to know?"

"I won't take up much of your time," I said. "Just tell me how you see the general picture. I'll dig out everything else myself."

He nodded and fished out another cigarette. "Hermann Gruss had been going to Oderbruch for treatment for about eight months. Almost everyone knew this, but no one is quite sure what he was being treated for. Oderbruch's nurse says there were never any records on the case and the doctor never told her anything about Gruss. Mrs. Gruss knew only that it was some sort of nervous disorder. The only medicine she ever saw him take was some pills. He must have gotten those directly from Oderbruch, for we've checked and Gruss didn't have any prescriptions filled during the time he was seeing Oderbruch."

"Illness might have been a cover-up for the meetings?"

"Maybe," he said, "but we don't think so. Gruss also had been spending an occasional evening with Oderbruch, on a social basis, so another excuse wasn't really needed. No, we think he was being treated for something—real or imagined. Gruss had obviously been feeling upset and out of the ordinary for several months. He'd been taking days off, even when his presence was needed, and often left his office suddenly in the middle of the day. On those days, according to Mrs. Gruss, he would come home and stay in his room, refusing to see even her. I believe there is no doubt that Gruss thought he was sick. Whether he was or not is another question."

"He was head of German counterespionage," I said. "What about his work during that time?"

"It's hard to be accurate," Farley said. "I suppose that it suffered somewhat since he wasn't giving it as much time, but the overall results obtained by his office were excellent. Right up to the last minute Gruss was a most effective anti-Communist. This is one reason we reject the Army's theory that he was a double agent. I'm convinced that the Communists would never have agreed to sacrifice so many important agents just to make one agent look good."

"Sounds logical," I said.

"The day Gruss vanished didn't seem any different. He'd been home the day before, but that day seemed better and went to the office. The men he worked with reported that he seemed nervous, but that was all. He went home at the usual time. He and his wife had dinner together, and she has stated that he seemed a little worried, but otherwise normal. After dinner he said he was going out for a while. Mrs. Gruss was used to this and thought nothing of it. At eight o'clock he showed up at Dr. Oderbruch's office. There was a patient with the doctor and he waited. After the patient left, he went into the office. About thirty minutes later he and the doctor left. They went to a café on Mehring Platz. They stayed there until almost eleven. According to a witness, they did a lot of talking, but there were no arguments or anything of the sort. It was fifteen minutes past eleven when Gruss arrived back at his own apartment. His wife was still up. Without saying anything to her, he went into his bedroom. He stayed there about ten minutes and left again, telling her not to wait up for him. A few minutes before midnight, a West German policeman saw a car with two men—whom he later identified as Gruss and Oderbruch—cross through a checkpoint into East Berlin on Linden Strasse."

"That's all?"

"Almost. But there are two things which contribute to our differences with the Army's theory. When Gruss returned home at eleven-fifteen, all he did was empty his pockets of all the papers he carried, including a book in which he had listed all of his counterespionage agents. On the other hand, Oderbruch's nurse had to catch up on the office records and worked until after midnight—after the time the two men had crossed over. But sometime after she left, Oderbruch returned to the office and cleaned out his safe. He also left the nurse her wages and a note saying that he probably would not return to the West."

"I get it," I said. "Once Gruss was over on the Communist side, Oderbruch's actions indicate he intended staying there voluntarily, while Gruss's actions at home would indicate that he intended to come back. The fact that he left his list of agents at home would indicate he had no plan for helping the Communists. But how do you account for the fact that he has helped them? And for the fact that he has apparently voluntarily made one radio broadcast and given an interview to newsmen?"

"That's the stumper, of course," Farley admitted. "But this is what I think—mind you, it's only a theory. I think there was either something wrong with Gruss, or Oderbruch convinced him there was. After treating him for a while, Oderbruch made him believe that his only chance of medical help was in East Berlin. Fits so far?"

"It could."

"Once they had Gruss along that far, they could make it a flat proposition. He could play ball with them and be cured, or refuse to and not be cured. In such a case, I think even a stronger man than Gruss might play along. If he thought, say, that he had cancer."

"Maybe," I grunted. There was nothing in the facts to upset the theory; neither was there anything to prove it. "What about Oderbruch?"

"Not too much is known about him," he said. "Oderbruch and Gruss were both part of the anti-Nazi underground and took part in the bomb plot against Hitler. They were the only ones to escape after it was over. Both were cleared of any suspicion by our authorities. Then Oderbruch took over this practice in West Berlin and apparently lost all interest in politics. He became fairly well known as a playboy. In fact, I think his lack of interest in politics is why there was never any complaint about his having a medical practice on both sides of the Curtain. I think maybe we slipped up there."

"Oderbruch could have been the double agent that the Army suspects Gruss of being," I mused.

He nodded. "Exactly. My hunch now—a little late, I'll admit—is that Oderbruch was a Nazi who managed to get inside the underground movement. Somebody tipped the Gestapo off to the bomb plot. Oderbruch and Gruss were the only ones to survive. It's a good bet that it was one of them. They did not escape from it together. Then, I think, afterwards Oderbruch went over to the Communists as a lot of the Nazis did."

"The same thing could apply to Gruss," I said.

"True," he admitted. He suddenly grinned at me. "It's only my theory. Proving it, one way or the other, is going to be up to you. Anything else?"

"One," I said. "I'd like a photograph of Gruss so I can become familiar with it before I go over. One of Oderbruch might help, too."

"Don't have any of Oderbruch, but I can supply the other." He picked up the phone and gave an order. A moment later a girl came in and put a photograph on the desk. He handed it to me after she'd left.

I saw the picture of a dark-haired, heavyset man who looked about forty. His face was handsome, but he looked as if he'd be a tough customer in a corner.

Farley slid an envelope across the desk. I put the photo-graph in it and stood up.

"Good luck," Farley said, holding out his hand.

"I'll need it," I said dryly.

He nodded in agreement. "Let me know if there's anything else you need. I'm sorry I can't go along with you."

I think he meant that.

I left his private office. From the girl in the front office I learned that Willi Borm and Henri Flambeau were both in. It was too late in the day to get started, but I decided I'd meet them. I tried the German first.

Willi Borm was a blond, Prussian-looking man of about forty-five. His hair was clipped close to his skull, his face round and rosy-cheeked. Despite a well-fed arrogance, the sight of my uniform brought him quickly to his feet. He did everything but click his heels. I didn't like him, but maybe that was merely my prejudice showing. I hadn't liked most typical Germans since I'd seen some of the results of their handiwork between 1933 and 1945.

I told him who I was and what I wanted. He fell all over himself assuring me that he would be ready at sunrise the following morning for the greatest honor of his life. But his cold blue eyes were studying me, probing for a soft spot. Back of their blandness something stirred, and I was sure it was a hatred and contempt for Americans. Or for everyone who was not German. I had run into it before.

When we'd fixed the arrangements for the following morn-ing, I asked him where I'd find Flambeau.

"*Der Franzose,*" he said, and for a minute the contempt was naked in his tones. But when he spoke again, he'd girdled his voice. "Herr Flambeau is one of our best men. He is to also help you, yes?"

"Yes."

"Es ist unglaublich," he said. "You Americans. You complain that we Germans are methodical, but here there have already been one hundred investigations of the one incident, yet now they send still another investigator all the way from America. Why not just ask for a report?"

"Maybe they're afraid something will be lost in the trans-lation," I said.

He didn't get it and it didn't even bother him. He was star-ing at me with a shrewd gleam in his eyes. "Perhaps it is something different this time," he said. "Perhaps the Herr Major intends to march into East Berlin, put Herr Gruss in his pocket, and return."

"Not me," I said lightly. "I'm the homebody type. I'll see you in the morning, Herr Borm."

"Leben Sie wohl," he said heavily. "You will find Herr Flambeau in the third office from mine, Herr Major." He watched me as I left his office.

Henri Flambeau turned out to be a younger, quick-moving little man who looked like an ex-jockey. His sharp face bore the brush marks of laughter. I liked him at once, but I was aware that it might be partly the influence of having just left the German.

"I'm happy to know you, Major March," he said when I'd introduced myself. He spoke English very well, although the words spilled over each other in a hurry to get out. "I was told to expect you. It will be a pleasure to assist you in your investigation of Herman Gruss. But why?"

"Why what?" I countered.

"Why another investigation? Why not merely read the reports which are already in the files?"

"I like to get things firsthand," I said.

He glanced at me shrewdly. "You are not a regular Army officer?"

"No. Reserve, recalled to active duty."

"Ah," he said. "And what do you do in private life, if I may be so bold?"

"A private investigator."

"A private eye," he cried. "It is wonderful." He cocked his head to one side. "So, Major, you are to be the simian who will pull the hot chestnut from the fire, *n'est-ce pas?* A chestnut named Hermann Gruss, eh?"

If this kept up, my mission would be as secret as a sunset. "Where'd you ever cook up that idea?" I asked.

"Ever since the good Gruss decamped, I have been sitting here saying to myself, the Americans are resourceful, they will send someone who possesses more courage than sense to kidnap him away from the Communists. *Voilà!* You are here."

I laughed. "I hate to disappoint you, but my orders are merely to make an independent investigation."

He gave me an elaborate wink. "Oh, yes, the security. You Americans must be very careful, is it not so? A Communist may be listening, and if there is, one can be certain that a particular American senator will be listening to the Communist listening. Yes?"

I made a certain brief observation about such a situation.

He drew himself up in mock horror. *"Le sénateur McCarthy,"* he said, switching to rapid French, *"dont le cerveau est une des grandes régions arriérées des États Unis."* He waited to see if I understood and he practically beamed when I laughed.

"I suppose Martin Lane doesn't understand French," I guessed, and saw I was right. I decided to change the subject before he got back to my reason for being there. "How come the CIA has a Frenchman working in its German office?"

"I will tell you," he said promptly. "I am very clever. Perhaps you have noticed. Perhaps I should be working for the French Intelligence. But to the French, all Frenchmen are clever, whereas the Americans are bowled over by the existence of a clever Frenchman. They are certain I am the only one. It is very flattering." He enjoyed this for a minute before going on. "Besides, I am an expert in the shadier characters and meeting places of Berlin. Yet I am without sentiment about them. There are many Germans who are also experts, but they are apt to be overcome by the tragedy of all those fine Berliners who were probably driven into a life of crime by our early laws against former Nazi Party members." He glanced at me out of the corner of his eyes. "You are fond of Germany, Major?"

"Not exactly," I admitted. I added, without putting any special meaning into it, "I just came from meeting Willi Borm."

"Ah, Willi," he said. "I have often thought you Americans might come to understand European politics—something which now baffles you—if you would only study Willi and me. If your Secretary of State would spend a month here watching the two of us, he would end up a far sadder and wiser man."

"How do you arrive at that?"

"It is simple. Willi is Germany and I am France. Willi is obedient to your every whim. He bows and grins and rubs his hands and clicks his heels and waits patiently for the day when the stupid *Amerikaner* go home and let him resume the course of his destiny. I, on the other hand, am impertinent, I make fun of my colleagues, I refuse to take orders when I don't like them—and I can hardly wait for the day when America will be so grown up no one can call her stupid. And there, my friend, you have the difference between Germany and France."

"Sounds good," I said, grinning. "I'll send a memo through channels."

He shrugged. "Since working for the CIA, I have become a champion channel swimmer.... I also have a short course in EDC which might appeal to your Secretary of State. Place Willi and me in a room together, put a gun in Willi's hand, and leave us alone. He will then learn why France is not happy about arming Germany. My only stipulation is that I be given a quiet U.N. funeral with no more than a twenty-one gun salute."

I laughed. "I'll speak to the Secretary about it the next time we're out on the town. Okay, Henri, I'll see you—probably the day after tomorrow."

"*Parfait,*" he said. "Just one thing, my friend. Bring some

American cigarettes with you—perhaps about ten cartons well wrapped up."

"Ten cartons? Why so many?"

His eyes twinkled at me. "We want to smoke out Hermann Gruss, is it not so?"

"You mean cigarettes still move briskly on the black market?"

"Just like the hotcakes." He frowned at me. "It is the cakes that are hot in your language, is it not?"

"Usually," I admitted.

He looked pleased with himself. "I am taking you to a café which is the center of black market activity. A man in an American uniform is an object of suspicion unless he has something to sell. So you will bring cigarettes, and the uniform will be ignored."

"Okay," I said, "but it'll certainly look nice on any Congressional investigation."

He had a suggestion about Congressional investigations. It was an excellent suggestion, although slightly unprintable. I grinned at him and left.

The CIA had made a reservation for me at the Derfflinger Hotel, which was only a few blocks from the offices. I checked in and had a couple of drinks and an early dinner. I was still tired from the plane trip, so I went to bed shortly afterwards.

Willi Borm was waiting for me when I reached the offices the following morning. He looked as if he'd been patiently waiting all night. As soon as I arrived, he put on his hat, setting it squarely on his bullet-like head, and we left.

"Frau Gruss is living not far from here," he said. "We will walk if you do not object."

"Okay," I said. We set off down the street, Willi marching stiffly beside me, looking as if he might break into a goose step any minute. I glanced down at him. "Were you in the army, Willi?"

"*Gewiss,*" he said. "It was necessary, you understand. One had no choice in the matter."

"Sure. What about the Party?"

"I had a card," he admitted. "But that too was necessary. It was impossible to do anything unless one was a Party member. But I was cleared by the denazification court."

"Naturally," I said dryly. "It was very convenient. All you had to do was go in and be washed clean of all your sins."

"It was only fair," he said stiffly. "There were many of us who did not approve of what Hitler did."

"What did you do about it?"

"It was impossible to do anything. He was the recognized government." He glanced at me, some emotion stirring darkly in his eyes. "While I did not approve of Herr Hitler, it was not as bad as it was always made out in your propaganda."

"You ought to try telling that to the six million Jews who died in German-occupied Europe," I said.

He pursed his mouth until it looked like a fat rosebud. "More of your American propaganda," he said. "Some Jews were killed, of course, but six million—that is fantastic."

"That it is, but not quite as fantastic as everyone trying to shut out the sight of six million bodies." I laughed without feeling any humor. "It makes quite a sight. Everyone in your country trying to forget those six million dead because every German knows that he shares the responsibility; and everyone in my country trying just as hard to forget the six million dead because we stood by and let it happen. So all of us are going to rewrite history inside our brains. And, you know, I think it's going to succeed. The triumph of mind over what matters."

"Propaganda," he said firmly. "Besides, Herr Major, it is no good to live so much in the past. We Germans must live only in the future. We must rebuild our nation, rebuild our place in the world. We have made progress, but it will go faster when—later it will go faster."

"When you can get rid of the Americans?" I asked. "Is that what you were about to say?"

He hesitated only a minute. "Yes," he said.

"And then?"

This time he didn't hesitate. *"Ein Volk, ein Reich!"*

"That sounds familiar," I said dryly. "But aren't you forgetting one small thing? The Russians?"

"We will get along with the Russians," he said confidently. "We are opposed to Communism, of course, but the Russians are practical. We will be able to make a deal with them so that Germany will once more be whole."

"I remember you made a deal with the Russians once before. It should be easy to make another one. You both want the same thing. All you Germans have to do is forget they aren't Aryans."

"Sie haben Unrecht," he said. "There will be none of that Aryan nonsense the next time." He looked very righteous, stumping stolidly along the street beside me.

The striking thing about his remark was the way he said "the next time." There was no doubt in his mind that Germany would someday make another attempt to rule the world; he saw no reason to even conceal it or be ashamed of the idea. There was no arguing with such a state of mind for words merely bounced harmlessly off the armor of arrogance. I knew from experience that there were a lot of Germans who agreed with him, far more than most Americans realized or would admit.

I dropped the discussion. I knew that if it continued, sooner or later I would underline a sentence with a short jab to Willi's nose. And then there'd be hell to pay. An American Army officer hitting a German could cause as much international excitement as someone dropping a bale of money over Russia.

A few blocks farther on, we entered a small residential hotel. We went straight up to the fourth floor.

"Frau Gruss is expecting us," Willi said.

He knocked on the door and we were admitted to what appeared to be a two-room apartment. We were in the sitting room, small and colorless, crowded with heavy, dull furniture. The woman who faced us was equally colorless so that her outlines seemed almost to fade into the woodwork. She was probably no more than thirty-five, but looked ten years older. She was a little on the heavy side, so that her body had lost most of its shape. Her blond hair was pulled straight back on top of her head. There was no makeup on her face. I had seen the picture of Hermann Gruss. He was a handsome, alert-looking man. It was difficult to picture him married to this woman. Maybe he'd gone to East Germany just to get away from her.

Willi introduced me and explained that I wanted to ask her some questions about her husband.

"Another one," she said in German. "Very well, Herr Major, but I can only tell you what I've told all the others."

"All right," I said pleasantly.

She waded heavily through the story she'd obviously told many times. I doubted if she had the imagination to vary it even if she'd wanted to. It sounded the same as what I'd heard in the CIA offices.

"Fine," I said when she finally stopped. "What I'm more interested in is how your husband had been feeling. You knew he was being treated by Dr. Oderbruch?"

She nodded.

"But you had no idea what was wrong with your husband?"

"No."

"How was this possible?" I asked.

She shrugged. "He told me that he had not been feeling well, but he said it was nothing important. He never offered to tell me more than that."

"How did his illness seem to strike him?"

"He was very nervous," she said. "It was not like him. He would be very irritable and at times he would eat hardly anything. It was the same with his sleep. There were nights when I would hear him tossing and turning all night."

"That was all?"

"No," she said reluctantly. "When it was the worst, he would sometimes shut himself in his room for a day or two at a time, eating nothing and refusing to see even me."

"What about just before he left?"

"He had kept to his room for two days. Then he went out that evening, after returning from the office, without telling me where he was going. As you know, he came back later but we did not talk. I could tell that he was very upset." She dabbed aimlessly at her eyes as though to wipe away tears that were no longer falling.

"Did it ever occur to you," I asked, "that your husband was suffering from some mental disturbance?"

"Oh, no," she said quickly. "There was nothing wrong with my husband's mind. He was brilliant. A little nervous, yes, but there was nothing wrong with my Hermann's mind. It was more like he was in pain and it was that which was making him nervous."

That sounded to me more like a thought that had come to her since her husband's disappearance. "There is also such a thing as mental pain," I said. "In fact, a neurosis may sometimes cause more pain than a physical condition."

"There was nothing wrong with my husband's mind," she said again. But she wasn't so certain of it. There was fear there, behind the placid dough of her face.

"What do you think was your husband's trouble?" I asked gently.

She looked relieved, but only for a minute. "At first, I thought it was nothing more than nerves. Life has not been easy for us. First, there were the days of Hitler and after that the occupation. Since then my husband has been fighting the Communists. It would not be surprising if a man was a little nervous. But since Hermann left, I have been thinking. It must have been something serious, something which frightened him badly. He must have gone to East Berlin for treatment. My Hermann would never be a traitor. Never! I have tried to think what it could be. I can only imagine that he has—perhaps—cancer."

She faltered at the end and then started to cry. This time the tears came, but now that they were real she did nothing to wipe them away. She stared at me silently, the two streams running down her face and dropping off her chin.

"*Seien Sie ruhig,*" Willi said sharply.

"No," I said. "Leave her alone. Tears are about all she has left. Come on." I led the way out of the apartment. Willi followed me reluctantly.

"Women are soft," he said with contempt.

I saw the expression on his face. "Americans, too, Willi?" I asked him.

"Yes." He bit the word off with angry relish.

"Only the men of Germany are hard and strong, is that it?"

He seemed to realize that he was admitting too much to me, so he didn't answer. But the answer was there, written in sullen lines on his fat face.

"Hard and strong," I persisted, "the way they were when they herded men, women, and children to the gas chambers? The way they carefully gouged the gold from teeth and stripped shoes from feet because the dead have use for neither? Is that it, Willi?"

"*Ich will nichts sagen,*" he muttered.

"You will say nothing," I mocked him. I knew it was useless to direct any of my anger at Willi, but it would take me a long time to forget the things that an army of Willis had done—and would do again if they got the chance. "Okay, say nothing, but trot along like a nice little master-race specimen, and show me the next witness."

We went out of the hotel and down the street in silence. I turned my thoughts back to the woman we'd just left. I knew it was doubtful I could find any new facts in going back over the same ground covered by so many investigators. I wasn't looking for facts. I was looking for the intangibles that might have been overlooked by the others. I thought I'd hit one of those. Freda Gruss was afraid that her husband was a mental case, although she'd never admit it. That brought up an aspect no one had mentioned. I didn't yet know what it meant, but it was there.

Fräulein Ursula Hamack was a different dish from Frau Gruss. A lot different. She had long blond hair, knowing blue eyes, a pretty face, and a figure that must have doubled the doctor's in-patient list. With Dr. Oderbruch gone, she was out of a job, but it didn't seem to be bothering her.

Willi told her who I was and she went through her paces. There wasn't anything there I hadn't already heard.

"How long did you work for the doctor?" I asked her.

"Two years."

"You probably knew him pretty well?"

"Very well," she said. There was a hint of smile about her full lips that made me suspect she'd known him even better than that.

"What were his interests?"

"Women."

"In the plural?" I asked.

"Oh, definitely in the plural." The smile was toying with her lips again.

"A pleasant enough hobby," I said dryly. I decided to get this part of the conversation out in the open. "I don't think you said exactly how well you knew the doctor."

She gave me an amused look from the blue eyes. "If you mean did I sleep with him," she said, "the answer is yes. Dr. Oderbruch is a very attractive man."

"With excellent taste," I said.

"Thank you, Herr Major." The expression in her eyes gave me the idea that she wouldn't be averse to a private German-American pact. The only trouble with it, I thought, was that it would probably be about as exclusive as the United Nations.

"But it makes me curious about one thing," I said.

"What is that?"

"I understand," I said, "that this was probably an arrangement of pleasure rather than love, but you do not seem at all concerned about the loss of Dr. Oderbruch since he went over to the East."

She shrugged. "It is more than a year since we were that intimate," she said. "I did not care to be a part of such a plurality. Since then Dr. Oderbruch and I were merely doctor and nurse. I have no feeling about what he has done. I will be able to find other employment."

"I'm sure of that," I said dryly. "I know that you have told other investigators that Dr. Oderbruch never gave any sign of being interested in Communism. Were you surprised when he went over to East Berlin?"

"No."

"Why not?"

She thought about it for a moment. "The doctor," she said finally, "was an adventurer, but only in a certain way. He wanted his adventure with a certain style—with luxury and power, if you know what I mean." I nodded. "So he would have gone anywhere, siding with anyone, if these things were provided."

"What about his professional interests?" I asked.

"He was in general practice, if that's what you mean. But most of his practice was with women—women who had a certain amount of money and had reached a certain age." She smiled. "The doctor's bedside manner was, I believe, most soothing to them."

"But he had no special interests? Psychiatry, for example?"

She hesitated. "He was interested in psychiatry, but I don't think he was too serious about it. Perhaps it was more like a toy. I remember that he often read in the field and he once made the remark that all the psychiatrists had overlooked the political possibilities in their profession. But he wasn't nearly as interested in that as he was in hypnotism."

"Hypnotism?" I asked. That hadn't been in any of the reports.

She nodded. "The doctor whose practice he took over had done a lot of work in hypnotism and left behind his library and notes. Dr. Oderbruch became very interested."

"Did you mention this to the other investigators?"

She pursed her lips. "I don't remember, Herr Major."

"Do you know if he ever used hypnotism on Hermann Gruss?" I asked.

"I'm pretty sure he didn't."

"Why are you so sure?"

"I overheard them talking about hypnotism once," she said, "and I remember Herr Gruss saying that he knew it was foolish but that he could never permit anyone to hypnotize him. I took special notice of it because that was the way I felt myself, and I had refused to let Dr. Oderbruch try it on me." She laughed. "Were you thinking that was the way the doctor got him to go over to the Communists?"

"No," I said. "I doubt if it would make any difference whether the doctor used hypnotism on him or not. A hypnotist cannot make a subject do anything he doesn't want to. I was just curious." I knew that was true, but I also knew if the hypnotism angle ever got out, it would produce some fantastic stories of how Gruss happened to desert to the Communists.

"Perhaps the doctor promised him some girls in East Berlin," she said.

"You think Gruss was like that?" I asked her.

"All men are like that," she said, tossing her head. "Oh, it was not that Herr Gruss suggested anything, but he had a certain way of looking at me, if you know what I mean. Have you seen his wife?"

"Yes."

"There you are," she said.

I laughed. "Maybe you have a point, Fräulein," I said. "Thank you for talking to me."

"I enjoyed it," she said. "If there's anything else I can do, please call on me." The way she said it left no doubt that she meant anything.

"I'll remember," I said gravely. I told her good-bye, and Willi and I left. Willi was in even worse humor than when we had arrived.

"You must not think," he said heavily, "that all Germans are as eager for occupation as some."

I laughed. "Don't worry, Willi. I'm not going back to see her. I wouldn't think of contaminating pure German blood."

He scowled, but let it pass. "What are you going to do now?" he asked.

"I'm through with you," I told him. "I have a little more work to do, then back to the States and make my report."

"But what are you going to do?" he asked stubbornly.

"Leave you," I said cheerfully. At that point, I did. I swung right on Wartenburg and left him. The last I saw, he was still standing in the middle of the sidewalk, scowling after me.

I didn't have much for my two visits. The only thing I'd gotten from them that seemed at all related was that Frau Gruss was afraid that her husband might be mad and that Dr. Oderbruch was mildly interested in psychiatry. It might mean something and it might not. I tucked it away in the back of my mind.

It was still early in the day, and I knew that I couldn't do anything with Henri Flambeau until evening. I went back to my hotel and napped away most of the afternoon. Then I made a neat bundle of my cartons of cigarettes and went back to the CIA office.

The Frenchman was in his office when I arrived, but looked as if he'd just gotten there. He seemed pleased to see me.

"Hello," he said. "And how is the M'sieu Cat's-Paw today?"

"No cat's-paw," I grunted. "Just a glorified errand boy with oak leaves on his shoulders. I'm going to see whatever you can show me, and then I'll head home and write my report."

"Ne me racontez pas des bobards," he said scornfully.

I grinned at him. "Where do we go tonight, Henri?"

"Business or pleasure?" he asked.

"Business."

"You Americans," he said with a shrug. "I am from Provence, and there we know how to live. Always pleasure first, then business."

"Provence?" I said. *"Il y avait un jeune homme de Provence…"*

"Dont les couilles étaient vraiment immenses," he said, coming up with the second line.*

We both roared with laughter and then we traded limericks for a while. That made us bosom pals. Finally, I reminded him that we still had work to do. He quickly went through a few papers on his desk. When he finished, he leaned back in his chair and lit a cigarette. "You brought cigarettes?"

I patted the package I carried. "Ten cartons."

"Good. I will take you to a certain café on Mehring Platz. You will be merely one American officer who needs to make a few extra dollars and so has the cigarettes to sell."

"What will that buy us?" I asked.

He held up one hand. "I have considered your problem,"

---

* The whole limerick goes like this: *Il y avait un jeune homme de Provence / Dont les couilles étaient vraiment immenses. / "C'est un grand avantage," / Disait-il, s"quand je nage, / Mais ça gêne quand je baise ou je danse."* The translation is roughly: There was a young man from Provence / Whose balls were truly immense. / "It's a big advantage," / He said, "when I swim, / But a pain when I screw or I dance."

he said. "There are many places I could take you. Dr. Oder-bruch was a great one for the night life. I could take you to many people who knew him, but it would be a waste of time. But the man we will see tonight is one from whom Dr. Oder-bruch bought many things in the black market. They were not really friends, you understand, yet they talked together a lot. And the doctor was a good customer. This man—his name, he says, is Horst Henckels—would be apt to check up on the doctor just on the chance there might be some money in it."

"You mean check up on him in East Berlin?"

"Exactly. He operates on both sides, you understand. Now, let us go."

"Who are you at this café?" I asked as we left the office.

"A big operator. One who deals in the black market on an international scale, so that what goes on at the café is much too small for me."

"I am flattered to be in the company of such an important man," I said.

"You should be." He chuckled. "It is droll, is it not? Now, remember, Major March, you let me do the talking at first and then just follow along. And leave the mention of Oderbruch and Gruss to me. I don't know what we will find out, but I'm sure it will be something."

"Okay," I said. "This Henckels, what does he deal in?"

"Everything. Forged papers, girls, narcotics, food, anything that will bring in money. Your ten cartons of cigarettes will be a very small purchase for him, but I will fix that."

Downstairs, we walked four blocks and then Henri hailed a taxi and gave the driver an address on Mehring Platz.

The café was like a hundred others in Berlin—small, dimly lighted, and crowded. It seemed to me as we entered that there was not a single empty table. I was right, but as it turned out, that was no problem. A waiter spotted my companion and led the way to a table where two men were sitting. He spoke swiftly to the men and they immediately left the table.

"The advantage of being what you Americans call a big operator," Henri whispered to me as we sat down. "In certain quarters, such as this, it carries more prestige than being president."

Henri ordered and the waiter brought us coffee and brandy. He waited until the waiter drifted away.

"Since we are at the meeting place of the black market, this is the best brandy money can buy," Henri said. He lifted his glass. *"Bonne chance.* In a moment, glance casually over your left shoulder. You will notice a small man standing beside a table at which there are five men. That is Horst Henckels."

I took a drink of the brandy and then slowly surveyed the room. Finally my gaze came to the table Henri had mentioned. The man who stood beside it looked the least Germanic of anyone in the room. He was small and dark, with gaunt, tense features. He was wearing expensive but inconspicuous clothes. I caught the glitter of a diamond as one hand moved in a quick gesture.

"It is said," Henri told me, "that Horst was one of the few men to spend seven years in Buchenwald and come out of it alive. He survived on hatred for everyone, guards and inmates alike, and so developed the art of personal survival to the highest degree. It is said that this is why he is the most successful black marketeer in Germany. I believe it."

"Jungle survival," I said, nodding. "If we want to see him, hadn't you better send word over to him?"

"Not necessary. You can be sure that no one enters or leaves this café without Horst knowing about it. He eventually comes to my table whenever I am here—possibly because he thinks I am the only one here who is his equal. But he would come no quicker if we were to send for him. We will wait. *Chaque chose en son temps.*"

We sipped our coffee and brandy and waited. The little, dark German drifted from table to table until he finally stood beside us. He hesitated, his gaze flicking from Henri to me and back to Henri.

"It's all right, Horst," Henri said. "Join us."

The German slid into the chair across from me. He was hardly seated before a waiter appeared with coffee for him.

"The Major is a very good friend of mine," Henri said. "You remember my telling you about the American jeeps I managed to secure?" The German nodded. "Well, it was the Major who arranged that little deal for me. He's a good man to know."

The German pushed the spoon around in his coffee and stared at me. There was no expression in his black eyes, but I knew he was weighing me, wondering if there were some way he could also use me.

"The Major," Henri said pleasantly, "has a little business to transact with you. Call it a sample, if you like. If everyone is satisfied by this one, then he might have something good for you." He nodded at me.

I placed my package on the table between the German and myself. He reached out and tore the paper at his end until he could see what was inside. His gaze shifted back to me.

"Was wollen Sie?" he asked.

"It's what you might want," Henri said before I could answer. "Would you be interested in a whole carload of this product?"

"You can do this?" the German asked me.

"If the price is right," I said.

He nodded, accepting it. In the world in which he lived, it was perfectly possible that an American officer might divert a carload of cigarettes. He glanced once more in the package on the table, then began to talk. He named a price and added swift details about where and how he would expect delivery.

I listened in fascination. German is a heavy language, lumbering over verbs and adjectives as a tank might roll through a mined field, but not with Horst Henckels speaking it. He was too impatient with his own language; he managed to twist it into explosive sounds.

"All right," I said when he had finished. "I will let you know the date of delivery within two weeks."

"Good," he said. He lifted his coffee cup in a way that indicated the business was over. He glanced at Henri. "How is it with you?"

Henri shrugged. "I can't complain. And you?"

"I keep busy," the German said.

"I guess even the loss of one big customer doesn't bother you," Henri said casually.

The German looked up. *"Was meinen Sie?"*

"The doctor. Oderbruch. I remember he was one of your best customers, but now he is over there."

The German grinned, but there was no humor in it. "I did not lose him," he said. "In fact, he is buying more than ever."

"Is it possible!" Henri exclaimed. "I knew, of course, that you also operated in the East, but I thought he might have trouble making contact. Or did he come back here long enough to arrange that?"

The German looked bored by the subject. "It was nothing. One of my best customers over there is Frau Schwabach. She is a very good friend of Oderbruch's. So it was easy. No matter who they are, sooner or later they come to me."

"So," Henri said in an admiring tone, "in that event you probably gained a customer. I imagine that now Herr Gruss can also afford to do business with you?"

Horst Henckels either didn't know he was being pumped or didn't care. "No," he said. "You know politics mean nothing to me, but it is my opinion that Herr Gruss is a fool."

"How is that?"

"He has been seen over there only when he is marched out to make a speech. Then he vanishes again. It is my opinion that they keep him locked up the way a banker does his money. Herr Gruss is a fool. He does the talking and Oderbruch collects the pay. But that's the way it is. The world is made up of smart men and fools. It is good. If it weren't for the fools, I would be a poor man. You, too, Herr Flambeau."

Henri changed the subject, and shortly afterwards the German paid me for the ten cartons of cigarettes and left. "Well, it wasn't much," Henri said.

"Not much," I agreed. "Who is Frau Schwabach? The name is familiar."

He grinned. "The wife of Heinrich Schwabach. He holds no office in the government of East Germany, but he is the most important Communist there. The power behind the throne—except for the Russians. So now you know one way to reach Oderbruch—for your report, naturally." His grin got even broader.

"Naturally," I said. "Let's get out of here."

He paid the waiter and we left. It hadn't added much to my knowledge, yet I couldn't help feeling that there was one more link in the chain. Frau Gruss was afraid her husband might be mad; Dr. Oderbruch had been interested in psychiatry; Horst Henckels thought that Gruss was kept locked up. Horst Henckels was only a black marketeer, but his sources of information were probably better than the police's. If Gruss was locked up and was still apparently willing to make speeches, he was probably not locked in a jail. It made an interesting train of thought, although it certainly was no more than that. And any attempt to follow it up would have to start with Oderbruch.

The next day I went over to the CIA offices and got some East German marks. I went over to the Gleisdreieck station and took the subway to the East. It was one of the ways to go in and out of the Communist side with no more than a casual glance from the guards in the station at the border. I got off at Alexander Platz and went into the HO store.* I bought several

---

* *HO* stands for Handels-Organisation, or Trade Organization, a state-owned department store of East Germany.

changes of clothes, everything from the skin out. When I finally came over to look for Gruss, I wanted to be sure I had nothing that would link me to the West. I took my packages and went back to the hotel.

I had made up my mind to go over the following morning. I got hold of Farley at the CIA and arranged for the rest of our plan to be put through. He would send through a routine code message to Washington, announcing that I had completed my investigation and was returning. Early the next morning, another Army man, about my build, would come to my hotel room in civilian clothes. He'd change into uniform and would then check out for me and be driven to the airfield, where he'd board an Army plane for the States. He wouldn't pass close inspection, but the way we saw it, there wasn't going to be one.

At about the same time, dressed in my East Berlin clothes, I'd slip out of the back of the hotel and catch a subway to the East. Then I'd look up my contacts there and get to work.

After I'd made the arrangements with Farley, I went back to my hotel and made like a man who'd finished his job. I had a few drinks in the bar and talked about leaving the next morning. Finally I bought a couple of magazines and went up to my room. I spent the rest of the day going over my sketchy plans and making sure I was going to be familiar with my new identity. I had papers proving that I was a German, currently unemployed but formerly working on the construction of the new apartment houses on Stalin-Allee.

Everything seemed to be about as shipshape as I could expect it to be. That evening I had dinner in the hotel. Then

I picked up a bottle of brandy and went to my room. I was going to have a couple of drinks and then go to sleep.

I had just started nibbling on the second drink when there was a knock on my door. I opened the door. It was Henri Flambeau. He was carrying a folded newspaper under his arm. He looked excited.

"The heaviness is in the fire," he said.

"What?"

"The heaviness?" He frowned. "No, that is wrong. What do I want to say? Oh, yes, the fat. The fat is in the fire. Ah, you have brandy. Good. Take a drink. You will need it."

"What the hell are you talking about?" I asked.

"This," he said, shaking the newspaper. "It is the late edition of *Tägliche Rundschau,* the official daily of the East. A friend just now brought it from East Berlin. Look." He opened it so that I could see the front page.

The headline, in German, said: *Jew Zionist Bourgeois Imperialist Agent in Berlin.* Below that was the story. It said that the Americans were sending a spy into East Berlin to kidnap Hermann Gruss. It said that the spy's name was Major Milo March and that he was now in West Berlin.

It had every detail about the plan. The only thing that was missing was a photograph. Maybe they even had that in their files.

THREE

There was a long silence while I stared at the newspaper headline and tried to weigh what it meant. A lot of planning had suddenly been thrown out the window by a sheet of paper and a little ink. Henri's copy of the newspaper had been acquired early, but it wouldn't be long before the thunder was heard all the way from a three star general down to the janitor in the CIA office. It ought to make quite a noise.

I tossed the paper on the bed and poured brandy for Henri and myself. The brandy washed out some of the bad taste my mouth had suddenly acquired.

"Nice," I said. "Looks as if TASS has a correspondent right in the CIA office. My own personal nomination for the job is Martin Lane."

Henri looked startled. "You're not serious?"

"No," I admitted, "but I'd like to be. If you have to find a son of a bitch, it's always nice to have it turn out to be somebody you didn't like from the beginning."

"There may be a spy in the office," he said. "It's always possible. You know, they've been training spies and sending them into West Germany at the rate of two thousand a month. Most of them are caught, but they don't care. On the other hand, it doesn't have to be a spy."

"Meaning what?" I asked.

"On something like the Gruss case, where dozens of trained men have covered the ground thoroughly and dozens of other trained men have already analyzed what they turned up, the appearance of a new investigator starts a lot of thinking. Almost anyone in the organization could guess that the man is going to be sent on a kidnapping errand."

"As you did," I said. I wasn't bearing down on it, but I was thinking about it.

"Ah," he said, "I can hear the wheels revolving. But you are right. You must be suspicious of everybody. It is the way one stays alive in this business. I can assure you that I mentioned my guess to no one, but you must take it with a grain of salt. Did anyone else guess your mission?"

"I have met four men in the Berlin office," I said slowly. "David Farley and Martin Lane knew why I was here. You guessed. So did Willi Borm."

"Ah, Willi. As you say, it would be so nice if the son of a bitch turned out to be someone you disliked. But in all fairness, I must say that Willi is not given to loose talk. But this does not leave us anywhere in particular. I am sure the entire office has been buzzing with gossip since you arrived. And the Communists have big ears."

"Big Ear instead of Big Brother," I grunted. "Well, the problem of who did what to whom is one that belongs to the agency, not me."

There was a long silence while both of us paid attention to our brandy. It was good brandy and well worth paying attention to in times of stress. The silence was broken by a heartfelt sigh from Henri.

"I guess that's it," he said. "You'll take the next plane back to the States and in about six months they'll try again. Maybe they'll have better luck next time."

Suddenly, I was conscious of having developed a personal interest in Hermann Gruss and what happened to him. I had begun to think of him as a victim—in a way a victim of two forces, one on either side of him—and I suspected that I was the only person who thought of him as an individual. To everybody else he was simply a symbol.

It had started out as a job, but it had become a personal matter.

"No," I said without even thinking anymore about it.

"No what?" Henri asked. He sounded startled.

"I'm not going back to the States. At least, not until Hermann Gruss and I are back here."

"But the office—they will insist on your returning and another man being assigned now that you've been exposed."

"The office," I added, "will just have to sweat it out. I'm going to go over before they've had a chance to give me any orders."

He threw up his hands. *"Dieu sait ce qu'il en sera,"* he exclaimed. "I admire your spirit, my friend, but I think perhaps you're a little light in the head. Your forged papers are no good. Your name is known. They probably know what you look like. And they'll be waiting for you."

"I'm going," I said.

"Dont les couilles étaient vraiment immenses," he quoted. He shook his head and switched back to English. "But how do you expect to accomplish this?"

I lit a cigarette and stretched out on the bed. "The way I

should have done it in the first place. You and I are going visiting. Then we'll come back here, and I'll change clothes and go over tonight."

"By tomorrow they will know that's what you've done."

"Probably. But they won't know where I am or what name I'm using. I'll have to keep out of the way of some of the Party members who knew me when I was there before, but I would have had to do that anyway. There won't be any leaks from this side, because, with one exception, you will be the only person who knows anything."

"You have decided to trust me?" he asked.

I shrugged. "I have a very simple yardstick. Anyone who knows the young man from Provence can't be a double-dealer. Spies don't have that much sense of humor."

"A philosophical point," he said gravely, "about which you should deliver a paper to your J. Edgar Hoover. Who is the exception you mention?"

"Horst Henckels."

"Ah, the papers. Of course. On the other hand, I, myself, cannot guarantee that Horst will not talk—for a price."

"I don't think so."

He lifted his eyebrows. "Why?"

"He wouldn't be in business if he talked," I said. "He must do a brisk trade in forged papers on both sides of the Curtain. If he talked just once, it would get around and he'd be through. He can be trusted because it would be unprofitable if he couldn't."

"Of course," Henri said in delight. "You are a man of genius. I only wish I were going with you, my friend."

"I wouldn't mind it myself," I told him. "But if anything happens to me, you can run over with a ham sandwich. Let's go see Horst."

We both tossed off the rest of the brandy and stood up. "We'll tell him," I said, "that I'm going over to the East to dispose of some other government property I've lifted."

"You wouldn't need forged papers for that."

"I would if I were careful. And I'm the very model of a careful major. I don't want to lose my oak leaves, so I go under a phony name. If anything happens, I'm covered."

He thought about it a minute, then nodded. "I think he'll buy that."

We were just going out the door as the phone rang. Henri looked at me. "The newsboy must have delivered the evening papers to the CIA," he said. "That's probably Farley."

"I didn't hear a thing," I said gravely.

He laughed and we left with the phone ringing loudly in the room.

The café was much the same as it had been the night before. Again a waiter led us across the room and a table was magically empty. We ordered coffee and brandy, and waited. Horst Henckels was several tables away, but he was moving slowly in our direction. We sipped our drinks and waited.

About ten minutes later, the little dark man slipped into the chair at our table. A waiter brought him coffee. It wasn't until the waiter left that he looked up.

"The carload has arrived so quickly?" he asked.

"No," I said. "I want to buy something this time."

He waited, with no change of expression. I had a mental

picture of him, waiting patiently there in the café for the whole world, buyers and sellers, to come to him.

"I have recently come into some other property," I said, choosing my words carefully. "We might call it heavy-duty property. I have reason to believe that I might get the best price for it over in East Berlin. The nature of the property is such that I want to be sure there is nothing to connect me to it. The risk of being asked for papers is small—but it's still a risk. I want new papers for the trip."

"It can be arranged," he said. "How much freedom of movement do you want while you're there?"

"Quite a bit."

He nodded. "It can be done. Because you are almost a colleague, I will give you a special price. Four thousand marks."

I nodded agreement.

"It will be ready tomorrow," he said.

"Too late. I need it tonight."

He hesitated.

"Eight thousand marks," I said.

For the first time I saw him show some emotion. For a moment there was cupidity in his eyes, but he masked it quickly. I suspected he was thinking that it must be a profitable deal if I was willing to pay double.

"Two hours," he said.

"Good," I said.

He hesitated again. "It is none of my business," he said then, "but if you would like a little extra insurance, I can arrange it for an additional eight thousand marks."

"What do you mean?"

"In order to give you freedom of movement, I will give you papers which prove you are an agitprop agent in East Germany, place of origin, Halle. That should cover you nicely, don't you think?"

I nodded. Agitprop meant that I would be listed as a Communist charged with agitation and propaganda duties. It was general enough to take me through most situations.

"This," he said slowly, "is also the guise used by most of the Russian agents who operate there as Germans. For an additional eight thousand marks, I will give you papers proving that you are in reality an MVD* man. The second identity card will fit inside the other, just the way the authentic ones do. I can assure you that every detail is perfect. It is guaranteed."

I thought about it for a minute. There were advantages. Considering the way the Russians operated, there was even less chance of being tripped up as an MVD man than almost anything else. They always had spies spying on spies, so that no one outside of Moscow knew how many MVD men there were around.

It was a good idea, but there was no point in letting him think I was a patsy. "Twelve thousand marks for both papers," I said.

His face got even blanker. It was the look of a trader. "Fifteen thousand," he bargained. "Below that I lose money."

I shrugged. "My profit won't stand that much of a cut. Thirteen thousand. That's as high as I can go."

---

* Ministerstvo Vnutrennikh Del (Ministry of Internal Affairs), Soviet agency of internal security.

He didn't look as if he was going to take it, so I threw in the clincher.

"In American dollars," I said. Dealing in the black market, he could always make an extra profit from the exchange rate.

"All right," he said. "It will take about two hours. You can wait here if you like or come back."

"We'll wait," I told him.

He nodded. "You want any special name on it, or will you take what we give you?"

I was about to say any name would do when I had a thought that amused me. "Make the German paper in the name of Links and the Russian one in the name of Nalyevo." *Links* in German means "left" and *nalyevo* means the same thing in Russian.

Something moved briefly in Henckel's expression and I knew he got it too, but that was the only sign.

"Make the first name anything, or just the initial M if that's all right."

He nodded and left the table.

"You handled that well," Henri said. "The only thing that might have struck a wrong note was that joke with the names. It was out of character."

"Nonsense," I said. "Even a black marketeer ought to be able to have a sense of humor."

"You'd be surprised how many people don't," he said. When he spoke again, he lowered his voice. "Not too quickly, take a look at the man in front of our table."

I glanced up and saw a heavyset German standing close to our table, but his gaze seemed to be fixed somewhere beyond us. He was fiddling with the buttons on his coat, then he turned abruptly and moved stolidly away. "What about him?" I asked.

"Part of Horst's thoroughness," Henri said. "Although I don't know why he has to do it in this fashion. That man was using a buttonhole camera and taking your picture. For the identity papers. But I don't know why he didn't just tell you that you have to pose for a picture."

"He likes the informal approach," I said. "Actually, it's probably just that even if he does something legitimate, he has to give it the cloak-and-dagger touch. I've known men like that. Some of them in our own intelligence. They can't buy a loaf of bread without making a production of it."

He nodded. "I'm sure that the papers Horst gives you will be perfect, but the price is a little steep. Are they giving you that kind of money to throw around?"

"I've got a little more than five thousand dollars in American dollars and twice that in East German marks."

He whistled. *"Pensez donc!* You must know where the body is buried. They do not hand out that sort of money in the Berlin office."

"They don't in the Washington office either," I said, "only they want Gruss worse than they want to look good in the budget report."

We ordered some more coffee and brandy and watched the black market life flow about us. Horst Henckels moved slowly from table to table, looking like a clammed-up version of "mine genial host," but we knew that he was probably conducting a major part of Berlin's mercantile business.

It was a little more than two hours before he returned to our table. He slipped into the chair across from me and slid an envelope across the table. I opened it and looked inside. There were two identity cards. The first one proved that I was a German agitprop agent from Halle. It looked pretty good. Even the photograph of me was bad, making it seem more official.

Then I looked at the second card. It was made to slide into little grooves on the back of the first card. It was an even better job. The red band of the MVD slanted across it. There was a minute description of me as well as a picture and a right thumbprint. I couldn't see anything wrong with it.

"Pretty good," I said. "Is that really my print?"

He nodded, and I thought I caught a glimpse of amusement in his eyes.

"How did you get it?"

"If it had been necessary," he said, "we would have asked you to permit taking it, but fortunately we were able to get an excellent print from your glass. It was a simple matter to transfer it to the card."

"I told you Horst was clever," Henri said.

He was clever, all right. Even I had to admit that. The only glass I'd had this evening was a brandy glass, and it was still on the table in front of me. He hadn't taken any thumbprint from it, but I decided to play them the way they were falling for the moment.

"We turn out the best work we can," Horst said in tones of obvious false modesty. "You will notice there is a place for your signature on the identity card. Do not forget to sign it."

I looked and saw the signature line. I also saw that I was a lieutenant in the MVD, operating throughout Eastern Germany on direct orders from Moscow. My name, according to the card, was Milo Nalyevo.

I didn't get it at first, then it hit me like a club between the eyes. I glanced at Henri, who'd been looking at the card over my shoulder, and saw that he'd gotten it, too. His thin Gallic face, usually alive with emotion, was drawn into an expressionless mask. I looked up and met the eyes of the German black marketeer.

"I took the liberty," he said smoothly, "of using your own first name on the card. Non-Russian given names are very common in Russia, and it will be much easier for you to have a name which you don't have to memorize."

"Very thoughtful of you," I said. "There's only one small question I'd like answered. How did you know that my first name was Milo?"

He shrugged. "It was nothing," he said.

"Of course, but I'd like to hear about it just the same."

"I think you'd better, Horst," Henri added.

The German looked at us, and I knew that in back of his blank expression he was probably laughing at us. "I must admit," he said, "that I was curious as to why a major of the United States Army would come to my café in full uniform. You see, I long ago discovered that my good friend Henri was innocent of ever doing more than buying his favorite cigarettes in the black market. Still, he did me no harm, and in a way I thought it might give me some protection to have a member of the Central Intelligence Agency consider me so important."

I looked at my companion, who was crestfallen.

"So," the German continued, "when he brought you in, I thought more was involved than the selling of a few cigarettes. It was then that I took the liberty of getting your prints from the glass that you held. I have certain contacts in military circles—purely as a professional precaution—and I thought the prints could be used to identify you. They did prove that you were not a member of the regular military group here. I called upon certain other sources of information and learned that a Major Milo March had just arrived in Berlin and apparently had something to do with Central Intelligence Agency."

"You are well informed," I said.

"I have to be," he said simply. "When I recalled that you had been interested in Dr. Oderbruch and Herr Gruss, I thought I had the picture. The appearance of a big story in East Berlin tonight, followed by your second visit here, seemed to round it out."

I studied him, wondering why he was telling me all this.

"Il nous a joliment trompé," Henri muttered.

"Maybe," I said. I looked at the German. "Were you the one who sold the story to the East Berlin papers, Herr Henckels?"

"I will be honest with you," he said. "It occurred to me. In certain matters of this kind, the Communists often pay quite well. But when I approached them, I learned that they already knew all about it."

"Too bad," I said, "but perhaps you can make up for it now."

His face took on a pained expression, but I knew it was only acting. This was a man who never felt anything except the rustle of marks in his pocket. "You misunderstand me, Herr Major. I would not do such a thing."

"Why not?"

"Not from sentiment," he said. His voice had grown harder. "Not because of my countrymen, who are pigs with short memories. Not for the Americans, the British, the French, who became heroic saviors only after it started costing them something. Not for the Russians, who are pigs with long memories. No, you may be sure, Herr Major, that anything I do will be for the benefit of Horst Henckels and no one else."

"In that case," I said, "why not collect what the Russians would gladly pay to learn that Milo March has become Milo Links and Milo Nalyevo?"

"You have paid me well, Herr Major, for those two pieces of paper, and to me the only thing sacred is the business contract which is profitable. There is another reason. I do business on both sides of Berlin. This is no secret. I sell as many documents to the Russians as I do to the West. They would gladly pay me for information about your papers, but thereafter they would not feel so safe in buying documents from me. I would lose more than I would gain. It would not be a profitable transaction."

I nodded. This fit in with the judgment I had already made of Horst Henckels. "But why tell us all this?"

"It would occur to you," he said. "I thought it better that we discuss it than have you go on your mission in uncertainty. Now," he added, his tone changing again, "do you find the papers satisfactory?"

"They look good to me."

"Then there is a small matter of thirteen thousand marks yet between us."

I took out my money and, holding it under the table, counted off $3,250. I handed the notes to him.

"Thank you," he said. He hesitated a moment, then went on. "As our friend Henri may have told you, I am not interested in politics. I spit upon all politicians. But I wish you success in your mission, Herr Major."

"Why?" I asked bluntly.

He grinned mirthlessly. "It suits my purpose to have Germany divided. I do not wish to see either side win. A unified Germany might not be so good for my business. The possession of Gruss gives the East a slight advantage. You will return him and the balance will be restored. *Guten Abend,* Herr Major."

He stood up and was swiftly gone.

Henri and I walked out as soon as he'd left. Neither of us said anything until we were outside and well away from the café. Henri sighed explosively. *"Pour l'amour de Dieu!"* he exclaimed. *"Ça c'est le comble!"*

"What's the last straw?" I asked him. "His attitude on politics or the fact that he was on to you all the time?"

"The German pig," Henri said. "I could have sworn that he believed I was a black market operator. And he did frequently give me valuable information. How do you account for that?"

"Probably gave you information when it was profitable to him in some way to do so. I imagine he'll continue to do that. He'll be just as valuable to you if you can get over the insult to your acting ability."

"I will cut his throat," Henri said fiercely. Then his expression changed. "But what will you do now?"

"Go to East Berlin."

"With those papers? You can't accept the word of a man like that. Those papers may be your death warrant."

"In America," I told him, "there is an old story about a gambler who went to gamble in a house that he knew was crooked. When asked why, he said because it was the only gambling place in town. That's the way it is with me. These are the only papers I have."

"You are filled with madness," he said. "Why not let them send someone else on this errand? It will be better for the success of the mission as well as for you."

"I'm going."

"But why? You are making a personal matter out of something that should remain an official matter."

"You are wrong," I told him. "That is one of the things wrong with our world, my friend. We let world politics become the concern of officials only, when it should be a personal matter with every one of us. Besides, what makes you think the Reds will be any less on the alert a month or two months from now? Or that they will have fewer spies around to tip them off to the new man that's sent? Why should I want to risk his head instead of my own?"

"All right, all right," Henri growled. "You are a stubborn pig of an American, but I am fond of you, so I will not argue further. Each man must go to his own destiny."

"I don't think it's so risky," I said. "The Russians will be expecting us to do just what you suggested. The last thing in the world they will expect will be for a man to come over tonight—and the very man they've just exposed."

"But the papers—"

"I'm inclined to believe Horst," I said. "I don't think there will be any tip-off from him. I suppose there might be a chance that somebody who works for him would do it, but I doubt if that's a serious danger. And I expect to take one other very slight precaution."

"What's that?"

"I'll tell you when we get upstairs," I said. We'd arrived back at my hotel. I led Henri around to the rear entrance and we went in that way. It had occurred to me that the CIA might have sent someone around to wait for me in the lobby when they didn't get an answer to the phone call.

The phone was still ringing in my room, but it stopped while I was unlocking the door.

"Persistent, aren't they?" I asked, grinning.

"They're trying to save your life," Henri growled.

"I'll grant Farley is," I said cheerfully, "but it's more than that now. It's more than three hours since you showed up with that East Berlin paper. By this time Washington knows all about it. And you can bet they're in a sweat, issuing denials that they'd send a spy into East Germany and hoping I get stopped so the denials will stand up." I took the identity cards from my pocket and began tearing one of them into small bits.

"What are you doing?" Henri asked.

"Killing off Herr Links," I said. "That's my other little precaution. The Germans and Russians are a lot alike. They have suspicious minds, but they expect skullduggery to be carried out in a methodical fashion. Once you start ad-libbing on them, they have trouble getting into the act."

"What do you mean?"

"If there is a leak, they'll be looking for a man passing as a German. Even if they know he also has Russian papers, they will accept the fact that he's only going to use those in an emergency. They won't be looking for a Russian. So I'm going in as the MVD man."

"Can you do it? Do you speak Russian that well?"

"Konechno," I said. *"Moyo imya Milo. Moya familiya Nalyevo. Kto tut govorit po russki?"* I started to strip off my uniform.

Henri was staring at me, his head cocked to one side. "Your accent is almost perfect," he exclaimed. "German, French, and now Russian. You amaze me."

"The advantage of a military education," I said. "The Army taught me all that back in the late war when they wanted to turn me into a snooper. Now I guess they're trying to collect an extra dividend on it." I slipped into the clothes I had bought in East Berlin. "Do me a favor, Henri."

"Anything."

"You'd better tell Farley that I went over, and you might add that you tried to stop me. But don't tell him what name I'll be using or about the papers. We'll keep that a secret just between you and me and the black market. Okay?"

"Anything you say, my friend."

"Then that's it," I said. I made sure I had transferred everything I would need to my pockets. "You might suggest to

Farley that since he can't do anything about getting me back, he might go through with the idea of sending a Major March back to the States on the morning plane. I don't suppose it will fool anyone, but why miss any chances?"

"I will do it."

"Good. Well, Henri, take care of yourself. I'll see you when the Gruss is in bloom."

"Wait," Henri said. His face was working with emotion. "We must arrange for a code so that if you need me you can send a message. What shall we do?"

I grinned at him fondly. I knew that if I really got in trouble, it was doubtful if I could get a message out or that he could do anything to help. But I also knew that his offer came from the heart and I wasn't going to throw cold water on it. "Why not a message left at Horst's café? I can always call from a public booth, and even if they tap it, they'll only get suspicious of Horst."

"Good, good," he said, rubbing his hands together. "What will the message be if you need help?"

"Suppose I say that the young man of Provence is somewhat smaller than he used to be?"

Henri was delighted with it, as I knew he would be. "Wonderful," he said.

The phone started ringing again.

"Give me two minutes," I said, "and then you can answer it if you want to. I'll see you, Henri." I returned the strong grasp of his hand and hurried out of the room, heading for the back stairway.

Down on the street, I headed for the nearest subway station

and got on a train going toward the British Zone. I got off at Gleisdreieck and changed to a train that would take me into East Berlin. While I was waiting for the second train, I remembered that just one other person had left the train when I did, and I wondered if someone had been following me. I looked around the dimly lighted station, but couldn't see anyone. I decided it was my imagination.

The train came along and I got aboard. There were very few people on the train at this point, and those were mostly heavily shawled women. They were probably from East Berlin and had taken the risk of crossing over to shop in the West.

The next stop was at Potsdamer Platz, which is right on the border of the two zones. More people got out, leaving the shoppers and me in the one car. I couldn't see into the other cars, but they were probably just as empty. A moment later the subway sped back into its tunnel and we were in Communist Germany.

For some reason, the notion I'd had back in the Gleisdreieck station popped into my head again. It was possible that I was being followed. I hadn't been too careful when I left the hotel or on the way to the U-Bahn. If the tail was clever enough, he could have remained out of sight in the station.

I got up and walked to the rear of the car where I could look into the car behind. There were three women shoppers and a fat German, his face buried in the newspaper he was reading. That didn't tell me much. I went back to my seat.

Originally, my plan had been to stay on this train until it reached Alexander Platz, where I would change to the Eisenbahn, which would take me out to the Lichtenberg area. That was where I was to meet my first contact. But now I'd started worrying about being followed, so I decided to check on it before I went much farther.

The train slid into the Spittelmarkt station and the doors slid open. I stood up and walked casually out onto the platform. I stood there for a second, not looking around, then walked toward a forward exit. The station was deserted, its rows of shops closed and dark. On one wall of the station there was a huge poster showing two Germans in the uniforms of the People's Police and the State Security Police. They were marching arm in arm. Below, in red letters, was the legend *Die Deutsche Volkspolizei ist das Blut vom Blut des deutschen Volkes!**

Behind me the train began clattering out of the station.

I reached the end of the shops and turned toward the stairs. As soon as I knew I was out of sight of the platform, I stepped quickly up against a shop and waited.

The train was gone into its tunnel and there was only a distant roar from it. Then in a moment I heard the other sound I'd been straining to catch—the thud of hurrying footsteps.

He came into sight, hurrying on his short, fat legs, the newspaper clutched under his arm, his bullet head thrust forward. It was Willi Borm.

I wasn't conscious of moving, but something caught his attention. He stopped suddenly and wheeled to face me.

"Ah, Major March," he said. "You are clever—but not clever enough, *nicht wahr?*"

---

* "The German People's Police is the blood of the blood of the German people." The Deutsche Volkspolizei was the national police force of East Germany.

I cursed myself under my breath. I didn't have a very high opinion of Willi's intelligence, yet I had let him tail me. I made a quick step toward him and he gestured violently with his right arm. There was a gun clutched in his fat fist.

"I wouldn't, Major March," he said thickly. "My superiors wouldn't like it if I shot you—but I would like it." He licked his thick lips. "I would like it very much, Herr Major."

FOUR

We stood there for a full minute, making our own little frozen tableau, while I studied Willi. I decided that he was probably telling the truth; he would like very much to shoot me. I had no intention of giving him that pleasure, but I also had no intention of being offered up for the pleasure of his superiors, whoever they were.

"I was right," he said, sounding terribly pleased with himself. "They said that once you were exposed in the press, you would be ordered back to the States, but it was my thought that you might try to come over on your own. So I took it upon myself to watch near your hotel. I saw you go to the black market place. You were there for more than two hours. What did you do, buy papers off him?"

"I just stopped in for a cup of coffee," I said. "The coffee was too hot and that's why it took so long."

"Stupid American pig," he said. "I know you went there for papers. There could be no other reason. I followed you back to your hotel and from there to here. Since you are an American Army officer and you are here in civilian clothes, there will be little difficulty in proving you are a spy."

"Aren't you the clever little double agent," I said. "Who pays you, Willi? The Russians?"

"I am a *Staatssicherheitsdienstmann*," he asserted proudly.

"One of Ulbricht's Planmenschen," I said. I put as much of a sneer into the word as I could. Ulbricht's Planned Human Beings. That was the name for them in the West and I knew Willi wouldn't like it.

Willi's face darkened with anger. "Enough," he barked. "Insults will only make it go harder for you. I will report everything."

"In triplicate, I bet," I said. "I'm beginning to think I under-estimated you, Willi. You're more talented than I guessed. You were a Nazi, and when they went down to defeat, you managed to twist around and land with both the Russians and the American Central Intelligence Agency. I guess you figured you couldn't lose, being on both sides."

"I work for the greater Germany only," he said. "You Americans would stifle us and make us live like sheep with the French. The Russians are more realistic. They will permit us to become once again a great nation and perhaps one day..." His voice trailed off.

"Perhaps one day the Russians will look the other way and you can cut their throats," I finished for him. I shook my head. "Willi, you Germans are living in a foolish dream."

"Enough," he said angrily. "Come. We go now." He waved the gun.

"Which way?" I asked.

"Back through the station. We will go out the other exit. Do not try anything, Herr Major."

"I wouldn't think of it," I said. I turned and walked back along the dark shops with Willi close behind me.

The station was deserted except for the two of us. From

ahead, I heard the rumble of an approaching train. If I was going to do anything, it would have to be soon.

"Willi," I said.

"Yes?" he asked suspiciously.

"How would you like to have a lot of money?"

"What do you mean?"

"I mean several thousand dollars—American dollars—and several thousand East German marks."

"Where is this money?" he asked.

I stopped and turned slowly around to face him. He gestured again with the gun, but I was moving so slowly he did no more than gesture.

"If you let me go," I said, "I will give it all to you." I moved my right hand toward my inside coat pocket.

"Stop," he barked. "This money, it is in the inner pocket of your coat?"

I nodded.

"I will get it myself," he said, "but do not try anything. At this range, I cannot miss, Herr Major."

He stepped in closer to me, the gun in his right hand almost touching my body. His left hand reached up to my coat.

I brought my right foot crashing down on the arch of his foot. As his body jerked with pain, I smashed at the gun and threw myself to the right at the same time. I heard the shot. The bullet screamed off the wall of the station, but I was too busy to congratulate myself on getting missed.

As the gun went off, I chopped across his neck with the edge of my right hand. His neck was too fat, but even so it staggered him. I swung my knee up into his groin. As he staggered back, I grabbed his right arm with both hands and brought it down sharply across my knee. I heard the bone crack, and his scream drowned out the thud as the gun dropped.

The train was already emerging from the tunnel. I had to finish him off in the next few seconds. I stepped after him and smashed my fist into the center of his face. I could feel the cartilage of his nose give way. Blood spurted down his face.

I measured him for the knockout punch, thinking I could then grab him and get him out of the station. He must have guessed that this was going to be it, for suddenly he tried to turn and run. He must have stepped in some of the blood that was streaming from his nose to the floor. His foot skidded. He tried to regain his balance, running in short, staggering steps that carried him blindly right off the platform directly in front of the arriving train. There was one short scream from him and that was all.

The train was screeching to a halt as I turned and ran for the exit. I knew I could barely make it by the time the train stopped, and the sight of a running man would be enough to send a dozen others streaming after me. I also knew it would be dangerous to run on the street above, yet there would not be enough time to walk casually.

I did the only thing I could think of at the time. I reached the stairs in a final burst of speed, was thankful that no one was coming down, stopped short, and wheeled around. Then I walked back down the stairs onto the platform. As I came in sight on the train, I brushed at my shoulder and stared angrily back up the stairs.

I'd been right about one thing. There were three men

running toward me from the train, and one of them was a policeman.

"Some fool," I said to them as they came up, "almost knocked me down. You'd think our comrades would be a little more considerate." On the chance that I might have to show my identity card, I gave my German as heavy a Russian accent as I could.

"Did you see him?" the policeman demanded. "Which way did he go?"

"How many different ways could he go on the stairs?" I asked, bearing down on the sarcasm. "Is this the way a German policeman catches a man—by stopping to chat? He was headed for the street. By this time, he has probably already reached Unter den Linden."

The policeman muttered under his breath, but the Russian accent and my arrogance had done the trick. He ran on, followed by the other two men. I went to the train. The passengers were already gathered around the front car. There were several policemen among them, and I realized that they were probably coming off duty from the Potsdamer Platz station. Three of them were down on the tracks with their flashlights.

"A mess," one of them said, finally leaping back on the platform. "The man is quite dead. He is carrying official papers. The train cannot be moved until we get him out of there."

There was a mutter from a couple of the passengers. "Can't be helped," the policeman said. "And you'd better all stay here. We will want to know what you saw." My little trick had worked so far, but there wasn't any point to seeing how far I could push it. I decided it was time to give my new identity card its first test. I stepped up to the policeman and showed him the card.

"I'm afraid I didn't see anything of importance," I told him, "and I am in a hurry. Official business. I trust it will be all right if I leave?"

He looked at the card and saluted. "Of course, Lieutenant. We wouldn't think of detaining you."

"Sorry I can't help you," I said. I turned and walked briskly toward the front exit. Back of me, I heard one of the other policemen address a question to the one I'd spoken to; he gave a guarded reply. After that there was silence—the uneasy silence that I suspected always fell when an MVD man was around.

I emerged from the U-Bahn station on Wall Strasse. A block away, I could see the policeman and his two volunteer helpers searching the street. I walked north slowly to Gertrauden Strasse and found a taxi. I told the driver to take me to the corner of Alexander and Holzmarkt Strasse and leaned back against the seat. I drew the first easy breath I'd had in several minutes.

Now that I thought about it, I didn't know what I would have done with Willi even if I had succeeded in getting him out of the station. His accident was the best solution for me that could have happened. But not one I would have voluntarily caused.

Within a few minutes the taxi reached the spot to which I'd directed the driver. I paid him off and waited until he'd driven out of sight. Then I walked up Holzmarkt until I reached the station of the surface railway. I went upstairs and waited until the Biesdorf train came along.

It had been two years since I'd been in East Berlin, but I found my memory of the city coming back to me. The address I wanted was on Siegfried Strasse, and I thought I could find it without much trouble.

It was a fairly long ride, but we finally reached the Lichtenberg station and I got off. Within five minutes I'd found Siegfried Strasse. Another five minutes' walk brought me to the house I wanted. It was an old frame building that looked as if it had been patched up many times. There was a sign in front that announced there were rooms for rent.

There was still a light in one of the rooms on the ground floor, although it was almost midnight. I went up and knocked heavily. After a minute, the door opened and a woman looked out.

My first impression was that she was middle-aged and plain-looking. But then I got a closer look. She was fairly young and probably beautiful, but a combination of no makeup and hair pulled severely back made her look older and plainer. She wore some sort of loose housecoat that gave her a completely shapeless outline.

"I'm looking for Frau Hedwig Schumann," I said.

"I am Frau Schumann," she admitted grudgingly.

"I'm Lieutenant Nalyevo of the MVD," I said. I showed her my identity card. "I want a room."

"I have no rooms left," she said and started to close the door.

I put my foot in the doorway. "There is a sign in front," I said.

"We forgot to take down the sign. The rooms are all taken."

"It is late," I said. "I don't feel like going back into the city. Nor do I feel like discussing the matter on your front steps." I crowded past her into the hallway. She stood there, still holding the front door open, and glared.

"Where is Herr Schumann?" I asked.

"There is no Herr Schumann," she said. "Perhaps you have heard that there was a war."

"I've heard," I said. "Now, I'll have a room. If you don't have one already empty, then empty one. Or I will do it myself."

"How long will you want to stay?" she asked.

I decided it was time to identify myself. She was my contact. "Until June seventeenth." The date of the East Berlin uprising was our code.

She looked startled. *"Berliner, reiht euch ein,"* she said uncertainly. It was the first line of the two-line chant used by the workers in that uprising.

"Wir wollen freie Menschen sein," I said, giving the second line.

"I don't understand," she said. "The evening papers had the whole story on the agent who was being sent. I didn't think they'd be able to get a substitute so quickly."

"They didn't," I said. "Same man, different papers. That's all there is to it."

"I don't know," she said doubtfully. "Why would an MVD man be staying out here? It's liable to cause trouble."

"I know," I said patiently. "I'll stay here tonight and tomorrow we'll work out something. I'd better be closer to the center of town, but I'd like it to be at least near another agent."

"Maybe," she said. "I was instructed to put you in touch with Rainer, one of our agents. He owns a small hotel on Schilling Strasse. Perhaps he won't object to your staying there. I will call him in the morning and see. But they shouldn't have sent you after there was a leak. It's dangerous."

"Just living is dangerous," I said. "You sound like an old woman. How old are you?"

"Old enough to know what I'm doing," she retorted.

I reached out and turned her face to the light. "You're a lot younger and prettier than you try to look. What's the idea of the two-pfennig opera technique?"

She jerked her face away angrily. "The way I look is my own business. Come, I will show you your room."

She led the way up the stairs. I followed.

"Is there really a Herr Schumann?" I asked.

"No, but he serves his purpose."

"And take that sack you're wearing," I said. I had watched carefully as I followed her up the stairs, and I couldn't detect even the slightest movement beneath its folds. "Or maybe I should call it a tent. It's obvious you can't fill it, but it makes me wonder how you could fill clothes that fit you."

"That's not the sort of undercover work you're supposed to do," she snapped. She stopped on the first landing and threw open a door. "Here's your room, Herr Nalyevo."

"My undercover work isn't so limited," I said. I came up behind her and then I gave in to the urge I felt. I reached out and patted her about halfway down the back of that voluminous garment. I'd been right. She was well rounded and shapely.

She whirled around and glared at me. "That," she said icily, "is not what is meant by making contact with an agent, Herr Nalyevo."

I grinned at her. "I'm supposed to be posing as a Russian MVD man," I said. "I was just trying to get into the part."

"Well, you were getting into the wrong part," she retorted. She turned and was gone before I could think of anything that would top that.

I went into the room, locked the door, and went to sleep.

I was up early the next morning and went downstairs. There were four typical German workers having breakfast in the dining room. There was a fifth place set, so I went and sat down. The Germans said good morning and went back to talking among themselves. I limited my response to a nod.

A moment later Hedwig Schumann came in. This morning she was wearing a dress, but it was one which managed somehow to make her as shapeless as had the housecoat of the night before. I remembered my discovery and grinned. She must have guessed what I was thinking, for her face tightened.

"What will you have?" she asked rudely.

Although the German workers did not look up, I knew that they were aware of her attitude toward me and were waiting to learn the reason.

"Kaffee," I said. *"Bringen Sie einige Brötchen und Butter und etwas Erdbeermarmelade."* I loaded my German with a Russian accent. You could feel the atmosphere in the room change. The conversation of the German workers ceased abruptly, although they were careful not to look in my direction at all. They hurriedly finished their breakfasts and left.

When Frau Schumann returned with my breakfast, I had the dining room to myself.

"Sit down and have coffee with me," I said. "Your other boarders suddenly decided that they might be late to work."

She went and got a fresh cup and sat across from me. "It was the Russian accent," she said. "It is like that all over Germany. Even the loyal comrades shake a little when they're around a Russian. We call it the Russian Dance. You are really an American?"

"Yes."

"You are clever," she admitted. "There are very few people who can manage to speak German with a Russian accent. Do you also speak Russian?"

"Yes."

"It is a good idea to pose as one of the MVD. Very few Germans will think of questioning you, so you will have to worry only about the Russians. Do you think you can find Gruss?"

"Well, I can try," I said. "Now, what about a place to stay?"

"I called Rainer this morning," she said. "It will be all right for you to stay there. His hotel is small and doesn't have many transients, but he says that a few Russians have stayed there and that it will not attract undue attention. He will be glad to have you. His name is Rainer Hansske. It is the Goethe Hotel on Schilling Strasse. I would go right away if I were you."

I nodded.

"One favor?" she asked.

"What?"

"All of us in this business take our chances," she said.

"Rainer is a good agent, but in many ways he is an innocent. I hope you will not unduly expose him."

"I expect to make very little use of him," I told her. "I will feel better for staying at his place. It will mean that my back is partly protected, but that is all I want. I may use him to obtain some information, but I expect to do everything else myself. There are some cases where one head is much better than two."

"Thank you," she said.

I finished my coffee and stood up. She also got up from the table and began idly clearing it.

"Frau Schumann," I said, "I am sorry about last night. It was an impulse—a most pleasant one, I admit—but it carried implications of disrespect which I did not mean. I'm sorry."

"It's all right," she said. "It was in keeping with the character you're impersonating. And perhaps I overdo my costume, but it can be dangerous for a woman in my business to be attractive. Mine is not the Mata Hari role."

She smiled and I could see that she was beautiful. "However, I must warn you—you are much too gentle. When a Russian does something of that sort, he uses a very firm hand." With that, she was gone. She was beginning to make a habit of leaving before I could think of an answer.

There was no point in sticking around just to get in the last word. I went through the foyer and opened the front door. I stepped outside and closed the door behind me.

The sound of the shot was thin and spiteful. On top of it there was a duller thud as the bullet hit the wall beside my head. Pieces of brick showered into my face, stinging like nettles. I dropped to the steps, trying to flatten myself out as much as possible. The gun cracked again. The bullet hit the steps and screamed away. There was a long, ugly scar in the cement less than two inches from where I lay.

Then there was only the sound of running footsteps in the distance.

FIVE

The door swung open behind me, and Hedwig Schumann looked out. "Those were shots," she exclaimed. "What—" She broke off as her gaze found me still on the steps. "What's wrong? Are you hurt?"

I stood up and started to brush myself off. "Only my dignity—I think. Both shots missed. I owe it all to the fact that I eat Wheaties every—"

"Get inside, you fool," she said. She grabbed me by the coat and pulled me inside. "The shots were fired at you?"

"If they weren't, the gunman was a terrible marksman," I said. "But the danger's all over. I heard him running away after the second shot."

"Your face. It is bleeding."

I reached up and rubbed my hand across my face. There were little streaks of blood on it. I got out my handkerchief and dabbed at it. "One of the bullets hit the brick wall and I got a few splinters," I said. "That's all."

"I didn't think anything would happen so quickly," she said.

"It must have been one of your boarders."

"Not necessarily. They would have spread the word that there was a Russian here."

"If I'd had any idea they'd react this way," I said, "I would have given my German an Irish brogue instead of that Russian accent. I didn't realize my talent was so fateful."

She laughed. "At least, when you get back to America—*if* you get back—you can carry the word that there are Germans behind the Curtain who resist."

"I can also say that they are bad shots. Do you think that was one of your group?"

"Not an agent, if that's what you mean," she said. "But there is a strong resistance group here. The Communists are well organized in the factories, but so are we. You might like to know that two Russian policemen were killed in this area last month." There was a note of pride in her voice.

"Now she tells me," I said.

"I will call someone who will go with you to the Eisenbahn," she said. "That way there will be no other attempts."

I put out a hand to stop her. "No. That would be a dead giveaway, for both of us. Just show me the back door and I'll take my chances. But you'd better get in touch with your friends. It may get a little rugged."

"What do you mean?"

"There's no way of knowing who's around spying for either the German or the Russian secret police, or both. As an MVD man, I've got to report this and demand that something be done. To do otherwise might ruin this whole mission. Can you ride it out?"

Her face had paled, but she nodded. "Who will you report it to?"

"The State Security Police. I'll go to the local office. But that way I'll be covered and so will you, if you can ride through the shakedown they'll probably give you."

"Yes, I see that it's necessary," she said. "It won't be so bad if you go to the local station. It's on Gudrun Strasse not far from the Eisenbahn. The men there are not exactly good Communists, and they will go as easy as they can."

"Good."

"In fact," she said thoughtfully, "perhaps we can turn it to some good. I will get in touch with someone and see if the shooting can't be placed on one of our enemies." In the casual tone of the remark I caught a hint of the steel that made her a good agent.

"You do that little thing," I said, "but first show me that back door."

She led the way through the house to the back door. She opened it and looked out. "I don't see anyone around," she said. She smiled. "Although I don't know what the neighbors will think if they see one of my boarders sneaking out the back."

"Just tell them Herr Schumann was coming in the front door," I said. "Although if they've seen you in that tent you were wearing last night, they'll never believe it." I left quickly while I still had the last word.

It was only a ten-minute walk to Gudrun Strasse and I had no difficulty finding the State Security Police station. A blond young man in uniform sat at a desk. There's no doubt about it; the minute you put a uniform on a German, he looks like a storm trooper.

The young man wasn't much interested in me until he got a good look at my identity card. Then he leaped to his feet, clicked his heels, saluted, and did everything but try to kiss my hand. Then he stood at attention, a painful look on his face, while I read him the riot act about a police force that would let an MVD man almost be killed on their front doorstep. When I got through, he practically fell all over himself assuring me that they would scour the city for my would-be assassin.

On that note we parted, and I went to catch a train into the center of Berlin. I took the subway instead of the surface train, and got off at the Schilling Strasse station. It was a half block to the hotel.

The Goethe Hotel turned out to be a four-story building, the sort that in Europe is known as a respectable family hotel. It bore the scars of the war, although it had been repaired better than many of the buildings in East Berlin.

I walked through the lobby, with its old-fashioned, plush-covered chairs, and up to the desk. The man who stood behind it looked to be almost sixty years old. His hair was pure white. He was small and his shoulders were rounded, although my impression was that it was not years that were responsible for that. Faded blue eyes stared with interest out of a face that was heavily lined. Again, I felt that these were laugh- and thought-lines rather than age wrinkles. He was a type of North German not often seen in Germany; most of them had left twenty years ago, and those who didn't had wished they had.

"I am told," I said in my best MVD tone, loud voice and all, "that this is a quiet family hotel."

"I like to think it is," the man said. His voice was soft and gentle, so that even the gutturals of German seemed to take on a poetic quality. "In fact, sir, when I first took it over and named it after Goethe, I had in mind those words from *Wilhelm Meister:*

Kennst du das Land, wo die Zitronen blühn,
Im dunkeln Laub die Gold-Orangen glühn?"*

"I can see the gloom," I said, "but I don't see anything that looks like oranges. Goethe was a scribbler anyway. For poetry, I'll take Pushkin."

"A good minor poet," the old man agreed.

"Enough," I snapped. "I have a lot of work to do so I want a quiet hotel. I guess this will do. Give me the best room in the house."

"Yes, sir. Will you sign the register?"

"Sign it for me," I said. "I'm Lieutenant Milo Nalyevo. From Moscow."

"Incognito, I suppose," he murmured, glancing at my clothes.

"When I want to be," I said.

He finished making out the card and rang a bell on the desk. A nondescript man shuffled out from an office back of the desk.

"Take over for a minute, Hans," the old man said. "I will show the Lieutenant to his room myself." He came out from

---

* Goethe, Germany's greatest literary figure, wrote *Wilhelm Meister,* a classic "coming-of-age" novel in several volumes (including *Wilhelm Meister's Apprenticeship).* The quoted lines are from a nostalgic song sung by one of the characters and were set to music by great composers such as Beethoven and Schubert. The words mean: "Do you know the land where the lemon trees bloom, where golden oranges glow *(glühn)* amid the the dark leaves?"

behind the desk and led the way to an old ramshackle elevator. He operated it himself and we went up to the fourth floor.

I followed him down the corridor to a corner room. He unlocked the door and stood aside to let me enter. I stepped inside. It was a large, pleasant room. I was surprised to notice that it even had a bathroom. Behind me, the door closed and I turned to face the old man.

"I am Rainer Hansske," he said. "Hedwig phoned me about you. I am glad to have you here. You are the man who was mentioned in yesterday's newspapers?"

"I'm the man," I said. I looked around the room. "It is safe to talk here?"

"Very safe." The old man smiled. "As soon as I knew you'd be coming, I started renovating the room next to this. It cannot be rented during your stay. Perhaps you didn't notice, but there are squeaky boards in the corridor and no one can reach this door without being heard. Somehow I never got around to fixing that floor. The result is ideal for conferences such as this."

"A good idea," I said. I sat on the edge of the bed and lit a cigarette. I motioned to the single chair in the room. "Sit down. Or will someone get suspicious if you don't come down right away?"

"Oh, no. It is known that I often wander around the hotel or get to puttering and don't come back for an hour or so. You might say that I am considered by guests and officials as something of an eccentric. I expect they're right."

"Cigarette?" I asked him.

He shook his head. "I never formed the habit. You are an American, sir?"

"Yes."

He sighed. "I once had hopes of visiting your country. In fact, I had a very generous offer from one of your universities back in 1935, but I fear I hesitated too long in writing my letter of acceptance."

"What happened?"

"Dachau." He gave me that gentle smile again. "My education was more or less completed during my stay there, but by the time I left, I was not so much of a specialist."

"What was your specialty?"

"German literature, more specifically Goethe. I'd spent my life learning and loving Goethe. 'And here, poor fool, with all my lore, I stand no wiser than before.' "

It sounded familiar. I thought a minute. *"Faust,"* I guessed.

His face lit up. "I didn't know that Americans of your age had ever read Goethe. I am happy to revise my opinion."

"My memory's a little rusty," I said, "but I can remember a little more:

Es war ein König in Thule,
Gar treu bis an das Grab,
Dem sterbend seine Buhle,
Einen gold'nen Becher gab."*

"Oh, yes," he said, nodding his head and smiling. "The King of Thule who was faithful to the grave. That alone, perhaps, explains why Goethe does not belong in the world

* The words mean: There was a king in Thule who was faithful to the grave, to whom his dying beloved a golden goblet gave. Thule represents a land to the north that is an unattainable goal.

in which we find ourselves and why even my countrymen are forgetting him."

I was curious about this old man. He certainly didn't seem to belong in the Germany of either side. "How did you happen to end up doing this?" I was referring to more than running the hotel.

"I can answer you in two ways," he said. "First, with Goethe, of course. In *Tasso* he said that talent is developed in retirement and character is formed in the rush of the world. Running this hotel is a form of retirement, while acting as an agent takes me into the rush of the world, so that I continue to develop a well-rounded soul." He seemed amused at his own answer.

"And the second way?"

"Before Dachau," he said, "I was a literary scholar. In Dachau, however, I became a philosopher. But it seemed to me that the modern philosopher must be active. This led me to my present clandestine profession. Which, I might add, has other compensations."

"What are they?"

"I'm an old man. Too old to go elsewhere and start life again. Yet the Germany of the last twenty years is not the Germany which I once knew and loved. I sometimes fight for things which are not valued by anyone else around me. Yet I am frequently in touch with others who do believe in these things. Goethe also said this quite well in *Wilhelm Meister's Apprenticeship:* 'To know of someone here and there whom we accord with, who is living on with us, even in silence— this makes our earthly ball a peopled garden.' "

I began to understand why Hedwig Schumann had asked me to be careful not to risk Rainer Hansske too much. "You feel your work is helping Germany?" I asked.

For the first time I saw sadness in his face. "No," he said. "Not to help Germany. To help individuals, perhaps, both within Germany and out. At least, I hope that my work does this. If you want my opinion, sir, there is no way to help Germany—unless we could start with the infants fresh from the womb. Germany is a sick nation, but how can you put a nation on a couch for therapy? My country has learned nothing from all it has been through. It is divided, yes, but each part has the same aim—to rule by force. It makes little difference whether it is called Communism, Nazism, or the New German Democracy." He seemed lost in thought for a minute, then straightened up and smiled again. "But you did not come all the way from America to hear the ramblings of an old man. What can I do to help you?"

"On the contrary," I said, "I'd like to talk to you about it again sometime soon. In the meantime, you know why I am here?"

He nodded. "To try to get Hermann Gruss back to the West."

"Yes. Do you know anything about him?"

"Nothing important. When I was told of your mission a few days ago, I tried to learn something. But there isn't much to learn. He is somewhere in East Berlin. He is undoubtedly a prisoner, but apparently a willing one. He only comes out when he is scheduled for an interview or a radio broadcast, and then he is heavily guarded. It would be impossible for one man, or even a dozen, to take him away from his guards."

I had expected this. "Then my best bet is to try to reach him through Dr. Franz Oderbruch. Know anything about him?"

"Dr. Oderbruch is another matter," he said. "He is a fairly important celebrity in East Berlin since he brought Gruss over. It is a role which the doctor enjoys. He is practicing medicine here, of course, but he finds plenty of time for night life with important members of the Communist Party. Perhaps I should say with the wives and daughters of important members. Do you know the Neva Restaurant here in East Berlin?"

"No."

"It is currently the favorite spot of the wealthier comrades and their families. There is a strong Russian influence, with caviar and Russian champagne and Soviet brandy, but I don't believe many of our Russian visitors go there. You will find Oderbruch and his crowd there almost every night."

I thought about it for a minute. "I believe," I said, "that my MVD papers will stand any examination that doesn't include checking with Moscow. I suppose I could go directly to Oderbruch on some pretext, but I'd prefer to reach him on a social basis. Got any ideas?"

"I imagine you'd prefer an indirect approach?"

I nodded.

"And you do not care what it involves if it is successful?"

"Not too much."

He smiled. "One who is always in the Oderbruch parties, in fact usually heads them, is Frau Beate Schwabach, the wife of the Chairman of the Central Committee. Frau Beate might be called Oderbruch's sponsor. She likes parties very much.

She also likes handsome young men, but not too young. It is my thought that you fit this description."

"I have only one virtue to give my country," I said lightly. "It strikes me that you wouldn't suggest this unless you had more and better reasons than the one you've given. What are they?"

"Heinrich Schwabach is one of the most important men in East Germany today. He is only Chairman of the Central Committee, but he has won all the recent ideological battles. You might say that every official here is temporarily in his pocket. His wife has almost as much power as he has, yet she is always striving to add important Russians to her group. A lieutenant of the MVD falls into this category. Her sponsorship has meant a lot to Oderbruch. He would not be apt to question anyone she took under her wing."

"Okay, then," I said. "We concentrate on Frau Beate." I thought about it for a few minutes. "Does she usually show up at the Neva at any special time or just drop in?"

"I believe they go there almost every night for the cocktail hour and dinner. Later they go on to other clubs and usually wind up at somebody's home."

"Find out for sure," I said. "Then, how's this sound? Could you get a group of toughs to attack her and her party just as they are about to enter the restaurant?"

He nodded thoughtfully. "And then she will be rescued by the brave MVD officer. A little on the simple side, but then Frau Beate is a simple woman. It might do very well."

"I like simple things," I said. "Then if anything goes wrong, it's easier to try to correct them."

"I think I can arrange it," he said. "You wouldn't want to capture one of the men to make it look better?"

I shook my head. "I see no reason why a man should be sacrificed. Let them all escape."

"Good," he said. "I will check on the situation and let you know. May I make one suggestion?"

"Sure."

"Go and buy an MVD uniform. You can have one made up by tomorrow. It will look much better than just waving an identity card in the air."

"It will also make me more conspicuous," I said.

"No more so than announcing who you are in a loud voice as you did in my lobby. And I assure you, my friend, that no MVD man would come to Germany without bringing along a uniform. He might have to work in plain clothes most of the time, but once in a while he would put on the uniform just to impress the natives."

"You're probably right," I said. "I seem to be waving this damn card around more and more anyway. Under the circumstances, it may be safer to be even bolder." I didn't think there was any real danger of a leak about my identity from Horst Henckels, but if there were, I might be safer in uniform.

"Good," he said. "I will have some information for you by this afternoon." He got up and shuffled out of the room.

I washed up and then went down and found a tailor shop. The promise of a little extra money made the tailor agree to have the uniform for me by noon the following day. I had something to eat and went back to my room to wait, taking a bottle of Russian brandy with me. If I was going to have to become a Soviet-type playboy, I might as well get in training.

It was late in the afternoon when there was a knock on my door and Rainer Hansske came in. I was stretched out on the bed, reading what passed for a newspaper in East Berlin and working on the brandy.

"Pull up the chair and join me," I said.

"I will perhaps have a small potion," he said. "No, don't get up. I'll get a glass." He went into the bathroom and returned with a glass. He splashed a little brandy into it and sat down. He tasted it and made a face.

"Have you ever noticed," he asked, "that even whiskies have political opinions? The Russians should stick to making vodka. It fits their character; brandy doesn't, so they make it badly."

"I've noticed," I said. "In fact, I was thinking that this brandy might well be charged with what Lenin called Infantile Leftism."

He laughed and took another drink. "I like you, sir. It is a pleasure to work with you. Most of the agents who come here never heard of Goethe, and probably not Lenin either, and would not know good brandy from bad."

"Spying," I said solemnly, "as a profession, has fallen upon sad days."

"Ah, yes," he said. "That is because we agents have become the fleas upon the body politic."

" 'A king there was once reigning,' " I said, " 'Who had a goodly flea, / Him loved he without feigning, / As his own son were he!' "

He laughed again. "You see, I told you that Goethe has a bearing upon almost everything. Although it is sometimes necessary to stretch things a bit." He finished his brandy and put the glass down. "Everything is arranged. It is rather better than I had expected. Tomorrow night Frau Beate has arranged to meet friends at the Neva Restaurant at six o'clock. She is not the most punctual person, but she will undoubtedly be there close to that time. Frau Beate is famous for a rather expensive necklace which she always wears. As she arrives, four men will attack her and try to get the necklace. We will make it criminal rather than political; there will be less reason for you to be concerned about them once they have been chased away."

"Good," I said. "Have another brandy."

"No, thank you. It is good to have my blood warmed, but I am too old to set it to boiling. You have seen about a uniform?"

"It'll be ready by noon tomorrow."

"Excellent," he said. "After the attack, the rest will be up to you. I doubt if you will have the slightest difficulty in joining Frau Beate's inner circle."

"I don't like the way you say that," I said. "What is this Frau Beate like? Fat, fifty, and feverish?"

"Feverish, perhaps," he said with a smile, "but for the rest, no. Frau Beate is perhaps thirty and looks less. She is the type of German woman that delighted Herr Hitler—blond and statuesque. It is true that her social life is beginning to add to her weight, but it is still well within the limits that are pleasing to the eye."

"You interest me," I said, "but not much. I guess there's

nothing to do but wait for tomorrow night and then it's in my lap."

"Precisely," he said. "But even after you have reached Dr. Oderbruch, you may not find it easy to get information from him."

"I know."

"You know," he said, "I am a contact man between the West and the agents of the West, so that I know most of them in this area. They are good agents, yet they were unable to find out anything about where Gruss is being held. That means it's going to be easier to steal the national treasury than to kidnap him. And if he's that important, any day they may decide to ship him off to Moscow. So you've got time on your back in addition to everything else."

"That's right," I said. "Make me feel good."

"I guess you knew how difficult it was before you came over," he said. He stood up and moved toward the door. "It's odd that I haven't heard anything from the West since you arrived."

I grinned at him. "You probably won't for a while," I said. I told him the details of what had happened after the story broke in the Communist papers. "If I know them, all the way from Washington to Berlin, everybody is scurrying around trying to prove they never even knew me. They'll come out in the open again when everything is over."

The old man was smiling at me. "I have a feeling, young man, that you will probably get Gruss and deliver him back to the West. I'm supposed to be only a contact man, but if there's anything I can do, you let me know."

"I'll do that," I promised him.

"I will see you later," he said. He opened the door and was gone. I could hear the boards in the corridor squeak as he left. He'd been right about my having plenty of warning if anybody tried to sneak up on me.

I spent the rest of the afternoon in my room. That evening I went out and had dinner in a little restaurant on Marsilius Strasse. Then I hunted around until I found a little shop that had some better whiskey than the usual Soviet brands. A thirty-minute talk with the owner about old liquors made him break down and produce a bottle of prewar French brandy. He sold it to me for a price only slightly smaller than the French war claims.

I hurried back to the hotel and used the brandy to entice Rainer Hansske up to my room. We sat around all evening, talking Goethe and cutting up other old touches.

The next day was just as quiet. At noon I went down and got my uniform. Back at the hotel, I put it on and tried to get used to the idea. It made me look a little like the doorman at the Astor, but I finally got so I could look at myself in the mirror without blushing. There was some of the French brandy left, and that helped.

Finally, it was evening and time to go. I arrived at the Neva Restaurant about 6:30. I was lucky. Right across the street from it, there was a small shop which also carried newspapers and magazines. I went in and bought a copy of the *Tägliche Rundschau,* then stood in front of the shop reading it. I did read part of it, but most of my attention was on the front of the restaurant.

The news wasn't very exciting. The big story was what a bunch of bastards all the non-Communist countries were and how they were trying to ruin Russia. Then there were a few stories on how wonderful Russia and East Germany were and how the workers of both countries had pledged eternal friendship. Inside, on page 5, there was a small story saying that the capitalist spy Milo March had been sent back to America after his foul scheme had been cleverly uncovered by the East German secret police. There wasn't anything about Hermann Gruss.

A big black Zis sedan pulled up in front of the restaurant, and I caught a glimpse of blond hair in the rear seat. I folded the newspaper under my arm and started strolling slowly across the street.

She got out of the car and the chauffeur drove off. At the same moment, four men leaped out of the shadows beside the restaurant and headed for her. They quickly closed in around her and I saw one of them reach for her neck. She screamed.

"*Budtye ostorozhny,*" I yelled. One of the men looked up as I dropped my paper and leaped across the street. He said something to the other three and they seemed to hesitate in indecision. They were doing a good job.

I reached the sidewalk and swung a glancing blow at the man nearest me. He rolled with the punch, so that it did no damage, although it looked as if I'd hit him hard. A second man leaped in and swung a clumsy blow at me. I warded it off and hit him on the shoulder so that it spun him around.

"*Beeilen Sie sich,*" the first man shouted. "*Kommen! Schnell!*"

With that, all four of them broke away and started running down the street.

"*Stoi!*" I yelled after them. I was thinking to myself that this was pretty simple and looked about as real as a cops and robbers chase at Minsky's burlesque theater. But Rainer had said she'd go for it.

I made as if to throw myself after them—thinking if only Actors' Equity could see me now—and then gave up with a sound of disgust. I turned to the blonde and let my eyes slowly widen as I took her in. It wasn't all acting. She was wearing a dress with a plunging neckline that stopped just short of complete catastrophe.

"*Vy ochen krasivy,*" I said.

She got it even if she didn't understand the words. She lost her look of fright and managed a smile that was obviously copied from some screen heroine. She wasn't bad-looking, although I didn't think anyone was going to study her face while she was wearing that neckline.

"I don't understand Russian," she said, speaking slowly as though she were talking to a child. "But I am very grateful to you for saving me."

"I said you were very beautiful," I said, switching to my Russian-accented German. "Pardon me, Fräulein, permit me to introduce myself. I am Lieutenant Milo Nalyevo, at your service." I gave her a stiff-legged Russian bow.

"Of the MVD," she said, glancing at my uniform.

"I have that honor."

"You must be newly attached to Berlin, Lieutenant. I don't recall seeing you before."

"I'm not attached to the Berlin sector," I said. "I am here on a special mission from Moscow."

"How thrilling. Is it a secret?"

"The mission, yes; my presence, no," I said. "I am sorry that the ruffians got away. Unfortunately, I did not wear my gun this evening."

"It's all right," she said. "I think they were after my necklace, but they didn't get it and that's the important thing."

I took time out to look at the necklace. It was quite a hunk of ice. It looked as if someone had certainly been sharing the wealth with her.

"I should have gone after them," I said thoughtfully. "I'm sure, Fräulein, that they were probably agents sent into East Germany by the capitalistic warmongers to make it look as if there were crime here."

"Possibly," she said in a tone that indicated she wasn't too concerned with the political aspects. "Incidentally, I am Frau Beate Schwabach."

"Schwabach," I exclaimed. "That is a famous name in East Germany. You are the wife of Heinrich Schwabach?"

"Yes."

"It is fitting that such a good comrade should have the most beautiful of women as his wife," I said.

She leaned forward to put her hand on my arm, making the neckline plunge even more. I would have been willing to bet she wasn't going to stay in it, but she did. "You are very flattering, Lieutenant," she said. "Where were you going when you so gallantly came to my rescue?"

"To the Neva," I said, indicating the restaurant in front of us. "It was recommended to me."

"Alone?"

"Yes," I said. "I do not know anyone in Berlin, and since I am on a special mission, I prefer not to mix with my fellow officers."

"You mean our German girls haven't discovered you yet?" she asked archly. "Then I insist that you join me and my friends."

"I wouldn't want to intrude...," I started to say.

"I won't have an argument," she said, putting her arm through mine and leading me in the direction of the restaurant.

Rainer had certainly been right about her. She was dim enough to fall for the trick we'd worked out without any doubts, and the way she was swinging that plunging neckline around, he'd probably been right about the rest of it. Inside, we were quickly seated at a large table. None of the other guests were there yet, but the blonde assured me that they soon would be. There were little pots of black caviar already on the table, with bowls of cocktail crackers. The waiter hurried over with a bottle of Russian champagne and filled our glasses.

"I wouldn't want you to think we're not hospitable to our Russian friends," she said. She lifted her glass. "Shall we drink to closer relations between the Russians and the Germans?" It had a mildly suggestive sound.

I clinked my glass against hers and we drank. The waiter refilled our glasses as soon as we'd put them down. I remembered that the Russians were great ones for toasts, so I lifted my glass.

"To German beauty, Frau Schwabach," I said.

Her hand was on my arm again. "Please," she said, "my friends all call me Beate, and I do hope we're going to be friends."

"To your beauty, then," I said.

We drank again. "What did you say your first name was, Lieutenant?" she asked.

"Milo."

"Milo? I don't know as I've heard it before. Is that a Russian name?"

"I do not know its origin," I said. "I believe my mother read it in a book." I was beginning to wish that Horst hadn't been so helpful in giving me my own first name.

"It's a nice name. I like it." She gave my arm a little squeeze. "I am sure that we are going to be great friends, Milo." She was a fast worker, this blonde.

Her other friends began to arrive shortly afterwards. There were two other German girls, Gerda Rogge and Hilda Richter. Both were rather pretty, but they faded into the background beside Beate Schwabach. There were two young Germans, both obviously minor officials who were flattered to be in the company of the wife of the Chairman of the Central Committee. Their names were Heinz Friede and Waltraud Dietrich. The fifth man to arrive was a Russian, and I began to feel that things might get a little tight.

"Come, Ilya," Beate Schwabach called as he approached the table. "See, I have a countryman of yours with me. You shall sit on the other side of me and then I shall be surrounded by Russia."

"Just the way it should be," the Russian said heavily. He looked at me with open curiosity.

"Milo," Beate said, putting her hand back on my arm, "this is Comrade Ilya Kuibykov of the Soviet Trade Commission. Ilya, Lieutenant Milo Nalyevo of the MVD."

"Zdravstvuyte, Leitenant," he said.

"Ya ochen rad s vami poznakomitsya, tovarishch Kuibykov," I replied. I was glad that I had learned Russian as well as I had.

"Gde vy zhiveotye?" he asked politely.

"Ya zhivu v Moskvye," I said.

"Please forgive us, my dear Beate," he said, suddenly switching to German. "I forget that you do not understand Russian and I automatically fall into it on meeting a countryman."

"I only wish I could speak it," she said wistfully. Her hand was still on my arm. I saw that Comrade Kuibykov had noticed it and was not too pleased. He turned his attention back to me, but stuck with German.

"Have you just been transferred to the MVD unit here, Lieutenant?"

"No," I said. "I am here on a special mission."

"Oh," he said expressively. "Which part of the MVD are you with, Lieutenant, if I may ask?"

I had already made up my mind about that question. I was sure it would be asked. There was nothing on the identity card to indicate my branch, so I had decided to make it the one that would stimulate the most respect and the fewest questions. "Special Squad assigned to the office of Minister of Interior Affairs Stakhanov," I said shortly.

Even the Germans knew enough to be impressed, and I was pleased to see that Kuibykov looked uncomfortable. Stakhanov was the head of the MVD, and the special squad assigned to him were the superhatchetmen. There was never any way of knowing whom they might be after.

Kuibykov seemed to lose his interest in questioning me further and turned his attention to the blonde between us. In the meantime, the champagne was coming faster; the two Germans were having a highly intellectual discussion about the history of Lenin's armistice with the German army at Brest-Litovsk; the other German girls, completely ignored, were seeing how fast they could get drunk.

Then the last guest arrived. Something about him made me guess that he was Dr. Oderbruch even before he reached the table. He was a medium-sized man, a little on the dapper side. He was dark and handsome, and beginning to look a bit shopworn. He walked with a stiff arrogance. It announced that he knew how important he was.

He came directly to the table, murmuring a greeting to the others but looking at the blonde. I saw from the brief glance he gave Kuibykov that no great love was lost between them. If I was right about friction over the blonde, Rainer's idea that this would get me close to the doctor was all wrong.

"A terrible day at the hospital," he was saying to her. "I'm simply exhausted. I think it will require a full bottle of champagne before I even feel human." He pulled up a chair and sat on the other side of me, which was the nearest he could get to her.

"Franz, darling," she said, "I want you to meet Lieutenant

Milo Nalyevo, of the MVD. Milo, this is Dr. Franz Oderbruch. I'm sure you've heard of him."

I managed to look surprised. "Oh, yes, the doctor's fame has spread even to Russia. I'm glad to meet you, Dr. Oderbruch."

"Hello," he said. "MVD, eh? I have a lot to do with your outfit. A very efficient bunch, I must say." He seemed to dismiss me and grabbed the glass which the waiter had just filled. He drained it at a gulp and held it out for more. He moved his head in a quick nervous gesture and looked at me. "First name's Milo? Odd name for a Russian. It might have made things uncomfortable for you."

I played it dumb. "I'm afraid I don't understand, Doctor. Is it a local joke? I arrived in Berlin only yesterday."

"His mother got the name from a book," Beate Schwabach said. She sounded petulant. "What are you talking about, Franz?"

"The spy the Americans were going to send over," he said. "His first name was Milo. I said it might have made things uncomfortable for the Lieutenant. But the spy was sent back to America." He drank his glass again. "Besides, the MVD is above suspicion. Even if the Lieutenant were named John Foster Dulles, no one would suspect him." He laughed loudly at his own joke; no one else joined in.

The champagne kept coming. By the time everyone was pretty loaded, dinner was ordered. As far as I was concerned, it was just in time. After dinner, there was a steady flow of Soviet brandy; then the party moved on to a nightclub.

It was quite a setup. Everyone ignored the other two girls. The two men with them kept talking louder and louder as they tried to impress the blonde with their political acumen.

She couldn't have been less interested. Oderbruch and Kuibykov were obviously vying for her favors, while she was just as obviously on the make for me. She was the only one really enjoying herself.

In the meantime, the brandy kept coming faster than we could drink it. By the time the party broke up at four in the morning, everyone was well stoned. I was feeling no pain myself. If this kept up, I would have only one stomach to give for my country.

When Beate announced that she was ready to call it quits, Oderbruch and Kuibykov leaped to their feet, jockeying to see who could reach her first. She waved at them and giggled.

"Milo will take me home," she announced.

"I was just going to suggest," Oderbruch put in smoothly, "that I could drop you off. There have been a number of things about the hospital which I thought might interest you." He turned to look at me. "Frau Schwabach is on the People's Hospital Committee. I'm sure you understand, Lieutenant."

I understood, all right. He didn't want to lose his position as court favorite, but he had to pretend he was doing something else. Kuibykov wasn't bothered by any of these fine points; he just stood there glaring drunkenly at me.

"Milo will take me home," she repeated as firmly as she could.

That was it. The queen had announced her decision and there was nothing for them to do but accept it. Tomorrow, if political fortunes changed, it might be different, but that's the way it was at the moment.

The blonde's chauffeur, I discovered, had been following

us and was now waiting outside the club. We climbed in and the big Zis shot away, leaving Oderbruch and Kuibykov staring after it.

We arrived at the Schwabach apartment without mishap, and I began to think that things wouldn't be as bad as I'd been expecting. The apartment was in one of the new buildings on Stalin-Allee, but when we got inside I noticed that in this case two apartments had been turned into one. The rewards of being politically correct.*

"Isn't your husband around?" I asked as Beate headed directly for the sideboard and poured herself a drink of brandy.

"No," she said. "He works at night. That's what they do at the Kremlin, and he likes to do things the proper way. It's a bore. Everything is a bore. Except you, Milo."

"Thank you, Beate," I said. "I think perhaps I'd better—"

"First," she said, "come here and help me with this zipper. I can't reach it, and I don't want to wake up the maid." She was indicating the back of her dress.

I went over and obligingly pulled down the zipper. I had barely let go of it when the dress slid down her body to the floor. She wasn't wearing a thing under the dress. She turned slowly, stepping out of the dress. "Make love to me, Milo," she commanded.

It seemed to me that I could hear General Sam Roberts reading the Articles of War as I picked her up and followed her directions to the bedroom.

---

* "The term 'politically correct' was coined in the late 1920s by the Soviets and their ideological allies around the world to describe why the views of certain of the party faithful needed correction to the party line." *Washington Times*, November 15, 2015.

SIX

It was eight o'clock in the morning when I left Beate Schwabach's apartment that first time. I reeled back to my hotel, my eyes feeling like prunes left too long in water, and hit the sack. At two that afternoon I was awakened by a phone call. It was Beate. She had to visit some hospitals and I had to go along. She'd pick me up in twenty minutes. There didn't seem to be any way of saying no. Besides, I was interested in hospitals.

My head felt as if the whole Cold War were being fought inside it. I'd been drinking, man and boy, for a good many years, but Beate and her gang made it seem as if I'd been attending tea parties. I fortified my hangover with some black coffee and a handful of aspirins, provided by Rainer, who enlivened the proceedings by quoting me more Goethe. It was something that started, *Wer nie sein Brod mit Tränen ass:* "Who ne'er his bread in sorrow ate…"*

"I'm not eating bread," I told him sourly. "I'm eating aspirin. The humble pie is for dessert!"

In spite of it all, I was out on the street, trying to make my bloodshot eyes look eager, when the Zis arrived. Beate was looking as fresh as a daisy, which made me feel worse.

The hospital expedition was a complete bust. They were the wrong kind of hospital. I tagged around after her and

---

* Another sad song from *Wilhelm Meister*, also put to music by famous composers.

looked at a lot of sick kids and men and women, but no mental hospitals. Between hospitals we stopped in for a few quick drinks, and my hangover began to fade away.

The rest of the day was a replica of the day before. We went to the Neva Restaurant. The same people were there—the two faded Party girls, the two talkative Party men, plus Oderbruch, Kuibykov, and me clustered around the blonde like three bees trying to get into the same flower. There was also the same flow of champagne. It looked as if I'd never get to find out if the Neva had good food; by the time we got around to ordering, I couldn't taste anything.

After the Neva, we went to a different nightclub, but otherwise the evening was the same. Every time I'd empty my glass of brandy, it would be filled again and somebody would suggest a toast. Or if they didn't, the conversation that swirled around me would drive me to drink.

The rest of the night was the same, too. At four o'clock, Beate insisted that I had to take her home. When we got there, we had a repeat with the zipper. The only difference was that this time I knew the way to the bedroom.

Again I got to the hotel at about eight in the morning. I was asleep while I was still a couple of steps away from the bed. I was awakened by a loud pounding on my door. I pried open my eyes and finally managed to focus on my watch. It was only one o'clock in the afternoon. The Communists, I thought, must have decided that sleep was some kind of capitalistic trick. My head was pounding until it was hard to tell which was the door and which was my head.

The knocking came again, this time louder.

"Just a minute," I called, wincing at the sound of my own voice. I climbed gingerly out of bed and put on some clothes. I went to the door and threw it open. The man who stood there wore a Russian uniform. An MVD uniform.

"Lieutenant Nalyevo?" he asked.

I admitted that was who I was.

"I must ask you to accompany me to the MVD office on Unter den Linden," he said. He was speaking very formally, but there didn't seem to be any great menace in his voice.

Even so, I knew there must be something pointing suspicion at me if a man had been sent to bring me in. I should have felt a little more nervous about it than I did, but my hangover was so bad that it muffled apprehension.

"I have your permission to finish dressing?" I asked, just as formally.

"Of course," he said.

I went into the bathroom and washed, politely leaving the door open so he wouldn't think I was crawling out the window. Then I came back into the room and put on my uniform. When I'd finished, I nodded to indicate I was ready.

We went downstairs and out on the street to an official car. He swung around the corner to Alexander Strasse and turned toward König.

"I had a rough time last night," I said. "Would it be possible for us to stop for coffee?"

"Of course," he said.

That made me feel better. Not only because I was going to get some coffee, but because it indicated the purpose of this call wasn't too serious. The MVD was not noted for addiction to Emily Post.

We stopped in the Alexander Platz and had coffee. I had two cups, but they didn't make me feel much better. I wanted to ask my escort the reason for this visit, but I ranked him and I decided it was better to pretend I thought the whole thing unimportant.

A few minutes later, we came to a stop in front of a large building, only a few yards from the border between the British Zone and East Germany. I recognized the building. It had once been Goering's Air Ministry and now housed, I knew, a part of the East German government. That made me wonder if Beate's husband was objecting to her latest playmate.

We went into the building and up to the third floor. The outer office we entered was occupied only by a young man in an MVD uniform. He nodded at my escort and we went through a door into a large private office. The man who sat behind the desk was probably about sixty, with gray hair and an Oriental face. According to his uniform markings, he was a colonel.

"This is Lieutenant Nalyevo, sir," my escort said. He saluted and left. The Colonel returned my salute and we stared at each other.

"Sit down, Lieutenant," the Colonel finally said, indicating a chair near his desk. So far the signs were good. "I am Colonel Netyrbay Nadashev, in charge of the MVD for East Germany. May I see your identity card?"

I fished it out and handed it over. He examined it carefully and handed it back.

"To what unit are you attached, Lieutenant?"

"To the office of the Minister of Interior Affairs."

He nodded. "Ah, that explains why you didn't report to my office. May I inquire the nature of your mission in Berlin?"

I knew enough about the MVD to know that I didn't have to answer that if I didn't want to—the beauty of claiming I worked directly for Stakhanov, the head of the MVD. On the other hand, the Colonel was being pleasant, so maybe I could meet him halfway.

"I cannot give details," I said, "but it concerns Dr. Franz Oderbruch."

"So that is why you are so much in the company of Frau Schwabach and her little circle," he said. "I had wondered. You look as if you'd had a bad night, Lieutenant. Would you like a little vodka?"

"Very much," I said.

He chuckled as he took a bottle and two glasses from his desk. "I've had reports on Frau Schwabach. She leads everyone a merry chase." He poured two drinks and handed one to me. "To your health, Lieutenant."

"To your health, Colonel," I said.

"Now," he said when he'd finished his drink, "we come to the matter at hand. I am sorry to bother you, Lieutenant, but it is one of those political things. We have a member of our German Trade Commission named Ilya Kuibykov. I believe you've met him."

"Yes."

"He is the brother-in-law of a member of the Central Executive Committee, which will explain the political aspects.

Now, unofficially, I am aware that Comrade Kuibykov has been interested in Frau Schwabach and that he is disgruntled because she seems to prefer you. Unfortunately, I cannot use my knowledge in this situation. Comrade Kuibykov has come in and lodged a complaint against you."

"What kind of complaint?"

"First, he asked me to have you transferred," the Colonel said. He poured both of us another drink. "When he found that this was impossible, he suggested that you were an imposter and demanded that I check on it. His reason for this absurd claim was your first name. By the way, Lieutenant, how did you come by your first name?"

I gave him the story about my mother finding it in a book.

He nodded. "I can understand that," he said. "There is a boy here in my command whose first name is Pierre because his mother once read a French novel. Perhaps we should have some sort of law against women reading books until after they have finished having children. But to get back to this imposter business …" He stopped and stared out the window.

To say anything might be to protest too much, so I said nothing.

"You can see it is a delicate matter, Lieutenant," he said, turning back to face me. "If I do nothing, Kuibykov's brother-in-law may feel that his prestige is at stake. On the other hand, too strong an inquiry might offend the Minister."

"It is a delicate matter," I admitted.

"It's kind of you to appreciate my situation," he said. "I have made a decision and I thought it only proper to call you and explain it to you. I will include the circumstances and the complaint in my regular report which goes to Moscow today. If you'd care to include a note on the matter, I will be happy to have you do so."

"No," I said. "I trust that the Minister's memory will not need to be helped." We both laughed at this little sally. Mentally, I was telling myself that sheer nerve is always the better part of valor. If I'd attached myself to any other unit of the MVD, Kuibykov's brother-in-law would have outweighed me and I might have already been in jail.

"We should have an answer back in four days," the colonel said. "I will show it to Comrade Kuibykov and we will then have an end to this nonsense."

"I'm sure that is the best way," I said politely.

"Well, that's that. Another vodka, Lieutenant?"

"No, thank you, sir."

He put the bottle away in his desk in a manner that said our conference was through. I stood up and saluted him.

"Thank you for your consideration, Colonel," I said. "I shall, of course, mention it in my first report."

"It was nothing," the colonel said. "These matters come up all the time. I often wonder why it is that members of the Central Executive Committee seem to have more relatives than anyone else. Come in and see me, Lieutenant, if there's ever anything I can do for you."

I thanked him and left. By the time I reached the sidewalk, my hangover was done. It was only partly due to the vodka. The seriousness of the situation had also contributed. I had four days at the outside—and it would be safer to figure three—to find Gruss and get him out of East Berlin. I'd already been there for three days without accomplishing more than a few painful drunks with Dr. Oderbruch. Something had to be done to speed things up.

I found a little café and had another vodka while I tried to think the thing through. I would need a little time to work out a plan for rescuing Gruss once I found out where he was. I obviously had to get closer to Oderbruch right away.

When I'd finished my drink, I went and called Beate. I told her that I had some work to do but would meet her at the Neva. Then I managed to suggest that I stop by and pick up Oderbruch on my way. She wasn't enthusiastic, but agreed that it might be all right.

I looked up the doctor and learned that his office was also on Stalin-Allee, at some distance from Beate's apartment. I made a point of going a little early, taking the subway to Marchlewski Strasse and walking the rest of the way.

The doctor's office was a pretty swanky layout. In terms of furnishings, it might have been on Park Avenue. It was a cinch that he wasn't planning on any trade union practice.

I gave the nurse my name and she came back to say that the doctor would join me in about thirty minutes if I didn't mind waiting. I didn't and sat down at the end of the waiting room. There were a bunch of magazines on the stand, but most of them were propaganda organs and I soon tired of looking at them. Then on the bottom of the pile, I found a couple of medical journals. I began leafing through them.

I wasn't actually reading, but just skimming the pages, getting an idea of what they were writing about. I might have missed the two articles that were under the head of "New

Drug Advances" if I hadn't caught a glimpse of Oderbruch's name. That made me look a little closer.

The first article was about something called lysergic acid diethylamide, or LSD. It was a drug whose special effects had been discovered by a Swiss chemist in 1938. One day, after he'd been working over the drug and inhaling its fumes, he handed in a lab report which mentioned that for several hours afterwards he'd been in a drunken state and had experienced weird fantasies. The next day, he took a small quantity of the drug by mouth; the fantasies were even greater. The chemist hadn't seen any special use for the drug, but he had reported his experiences anyway. Word of it had spread throughout the world of science.

The next step had been taken by an American doctor—and I was surprised that they gave him credit. Dr. Max Rinkel, a researcher in psychiatry, had obtained the drug and carried on experiments. The result was that they soon discovered the drug would produce all the major symptoms of schizo-phrenia in a completely healthy man. After several hours, the drug would wear off and the man would be normal again. The American doctor thought the value of the drug lay in the fact that it enabled psychoanalysts and psychiatrists to learn about schizophrenia by giving it to themselves for a short time, and in enabling them to uncover incipient cases of schizophrenia at a time when treatment could be the most effective.

The next important step, according to the article, and here was where it suddenly got coy, had recently been made by Dr. Franz Oderbruch of East Berlin. It never got around to saying what Dr. Oderbruch had done with lysergic acid diethylamide, but it said that his experiments would be invaluable to the People's Governments of the world. The Institute of Soviet Science, it added, was giving an award to Dr. Oderbruch.

The second article was a brief one on chlorpromazine. This seemed to be a wonder drug with all the healing claims of the old-fashioned horse liniment. According to the article, it gave great relief in cases of anxiety, depression, schizophrenia, dizziness, nervous stomach, alcoholism, hangovers, and insomnia. Everything but falling hair.

There was no mention of Oderbruch, so I lost interest in the article even before I finished it.

I put the magazine down and waited for the doctor, idly thinking about all the new drugs that were popping up. The old family doctor could do anything from making you happy to making you crazy. Something clicked in my brain and I sat up a little straighter. The only idea about Gruss that had occurred to me was that he had some sort of mental illness. And here was an article saying that Oderbruch was one of the foremost experimenters with a drug that could cause mental illness. I didn't believe in coincidences, and here was one that would choke an elephant. I began to get the excitement that comes with knowing that you're getting close.

A few minutes later the nurse motioned for me to go in to see the doctor. I went through the door and found him in the examination room.

"How are you, Lieutenant," he said pleasantly. "Is this a professional call?"

"No," I said. "Beate said that you're always showing up late. She suggested that I drop by and collect you this time so you won't forget to leave the office."

"Did she really?" he asked. He seemed very pleased. "Maybe I have been working pretty hard, but there is so much work to be done. But I guess there aren't any more patients for today and there's no reason why I can't leave now." He began taking off his white coat. "How do you like our city by now, Lieutenant?"

"Fine," I said. "It's not Moscow, but then some of that feeling may come from not knowing Berlin."

"Beate will see that you get acquainted with it. By the way, Lieutenant, man to man, what do you think of our Beate?"

"She's a very attractive woman," I said cautiously.

"Yes, yes," he said impatiently. From his tone, I realized that he had less interest in hearing my opinion than in giving his own. "Her position is, of course, quite important because of her husband. She has done a great deal for me and I expect her to help my career even further. You see, I am frank with you. She can do a lot for someone when she is interested."

"I suppose she can," I said. I hoped my tone indicated that I wasn't interested in having a lot done for me.

"Of course, Beate is often interested in a number of men at the same time," he said. He glanced at me keenly. "You have realized that our Beate is a nymphomaniac?"

"Sure," I said. If I sounded tired it was because I was. "Just what every little boy wants to find under his Christmas tree."

Oderbruch laughed. "I can see you're a man of the world, Lieutenant," he said. "Personally, my own experience has taught me that every man wants a nymphomaniac until he gets one. Then he begins to long for a monastery. Frankly, I'm rather glad you came along. It is difficult to keep up with Beate and one's work." He had his coat on and we started to leave.

"So I'm discovering," I said as we went through the waiting room.

"Oh, are you here on an official mission, Lieutenant? I thought perhaps you were on vacation."

"No. Fortunately, as it has turned out, I'm able, to some degree, to combine my mission and my relaxing."

"Oh?" I could see the wheels turning around in his head as he tried to guess what kind of work an MVD man could be doing at Beate's parties. If there were any shadow on his patroness, he'd want to know about it. But he tried to sound casual as he probed. "Is it a secret mission, or is it permitted to ask what it is?"

I decided to make him happy. "It's secret, although rather routine. We have reason to believe that a check is needed on certain of our own people who are attached to various missions here. That is all." I knew that he would connect this up with Kuibykov. It might even make him feel more friendly to me, since he didn't like the Russian.

"I see," he said thoughtfully. "I suppose there must be problems like that. If there's ever anything I can do to help you, Lieutenant, please feel free to call upon me. I think you will find that I have a record of being most cooperative."

"I'm sure you do," I said.

"You know," he said in confidential tones, "I was the one

responsible for getting Hermann Gruss out of West Berlin and I'm handling that situation for the government."

"I remember hearing about it," I said politely.

We reached his car and started driving to the Neva. Oderbruch drove with a careless arrogance. A dozen times I found myself trying to help him brake by pressing down on the floorboard with my right foot. It was, I thought, one thing that a lot of Germans had in common with the Russians; they drove with an almost complete disregard for others.

Beate and the rest were already at the Neva when we arrived. Two minutes after we got there, we were tonsil-deep in the usual Soviet champagne. This night was going to be no different from other nights. Except that I was determined to make it different in one respect.

I waited until later when we were at the nightclub and everybody was a little bit loaded. Beate had finally consented to dance with Kuibykov and they were out on the dance floor. Kuibykov moved like a bear in the mating season, and Beate's dancing could only be described as wriggling. Oderbruch was watching them with a gloomy expression.

"It's enough to make one lose belief in the terpsichorean arts," I said to him.

He nodded. "The only thing that bothers me," he said, "is that I think he's trying to sell her on some project of his which would interfere with one of mine. Beate is very influential in hospital work, and it is largely because of her support that I've been able to do as much as I have. Normally, I wouldn't fear her switching that support, but, as you probably know, Kuibykov has very good connections back in Russia. Beate will have that in mind."

"He is well connected," I said. "But it's always possible that he will not continue to be in a position to threaten your project."

He got the meaning I intended him to. His face brightened as he looked at me. I could see he wanted to ask questions, but didn't quite dare.

"While I was waiting for you this afternoon," I said casually, "I was leafing through a medical journal in your office. I was surprised to see that you've done a lot of work with mental illness."

"Yes, I have."

"In Russia," I said, with a smile, "we are inclined to think that psychiatry is mostly capitalistic nonsense. Man is formed by his economic state, not by what his father said to him."

"That is mostly true," Oderbruch said. "The study of psychiatry in the capitalistic countries has taken the form of pampering the rich and the parasites. But there is a political aspect to the study of psychiatry which has been ignored. It is this which has interested me. In connection with it, the discovery of many of the new drugs opened entirely new avenues of experimentation."

"You are carrying on your experiments?"

"Oh, yes." He seemed eager to discuss his work, yet obviously felt that he had to hold back. He glanced absent-mindedly at my uniform, and I could almost see him thinking that it was safe to talk a little more. "I don't suppose you've heard of the New Lenin Hospital?"

"No."

"It's not surprising. Very few know of it outside of inner

Party circles. It is a new hospital built only a few months ago on Treskow Allee, near Schloss Park. I am in charge there."

"And it is there that you carry on your experiments?" I asked.

He nodded. "We are carrying on a number of important experiments at the hospital. Many of them promise to be invaluable to our cause. I expect to give a complete report on what we've been doing to the Institute of Soviet Science within a few months. It will be a great day for international Communism." Those were his words, but the tone implied that it would be a great day for Dr. Oderbruch.

"Gruss?" I asked.

He frowned. "Gruss is part of the experiment, of course, but he is not that important. I don't mean to underestimate the importance he has, you understand. You appreciate the fact that while Gruss did come to us voluntarily, he is not voluntarily giving us any information. Yet he possesses a lot of important information, not only in regard to West Germany but also concerning methods and plans of the United States. I have no doubt that he will eventually tell us all he knows. It is a matter of great interest to your department, Lieutenant, even though it is not our most important work."

"I can see that," I said. I noticed he was looking a little nervous, as though realizing he might have talked too much, so I switched the conversation.

"You have been in the Party long, Doctor?"

He was relieved at the change. "Since 1934," he said proudly.

"Then you went through some difficult times," I said,

letting my voice show admiration. "It must not have been easy in those years in Germany. You must have also taken part in the July twentieth bomb plot against Hitler."

He laughed. "In more ways than one," he said. "I was in on that in three different ways."

I looked at him questioningly.

"I was a member of the Party then," he said, "and a member of the German underground. In addition, under orders from the Party, I was also a member of the Nazi Party. It was finally decided by our Party that nothing would be gained by assassinating Hitler; in fact, much might be lost. I was instructed to inform the Nazi Party of the plot at the last minute. I did so, with the results you know. You know how those things are worked out."

"Of course. Everything must be looked at in its historical reference," I said solemnly. "It seems to me I recall reading that Gruss was in that, too."

"Oh, yes. He and I were the only ones to escape. I don't quite know how he managed. Many people in the West think that Gruss was the double agent who tipped off the Nazis." He laughed.

"That was very clever of you," I said flatly.

Beate and Kuibykov returned to the table, ending our conversation, but I was satisfied. I was sure that I knew where they had Gruss, and I couldn't expect to get any more out of Oderbruch.

The rest of the night went according to schedule. The party broke up at four. This time I didn't even have to wait for my cue. I went wearily across the room to unzip Beate as soon as we were in the apartment.

SEVEN

One day of my three was gone. In two more days, the answer from Moscow could be feared any minute, and a guy named Milo Nalyevo, maiden name March, had better be hard to find. I had no desire to be an international incident; my ambitions were a little more in the direction of slippers under the chair and the home fires burning. And I was almost as anxious to get away from Beate as I was to stay away from the Russians.

I hadn't gotten to bed any earlier than the first two party nights, but I was up that day by noon without being called out of the sack by either Beate or the MVD. It wasn't easy. I didn't really get my eyes opened until after I'd had a cold shower. A cup of strong black coffee and four aspirins helped a little more, but I didn't begin to feel anywhere near human until I finally gave in and had a couple of drinks in the nearest bar. If this assignment lasted much longer, it would be a question of who killed me first, the Russians or a hangover.

After some deliberation, I decided to run my first errand in plain clothes. In one way the uniform might be safer, but it would also be more conspicuous, and that was the state I desired least.

I walked to the end of the street and caught a subway at the Schilling Strasse station. I rode to the end of the line, getting off at the Betriebs station. I was the only passenger when we reached it, but nobody paid any attention to me as I cut across to Treskow Allee. I turned right and went down to the end of Schloss Park, then turned left and walked around the park looking for the hospital.

They'd built it at the very edge of the park. It was a big, impressive-looking building, set in a good ten acres of land. Around it there was a solid brick wall at least ten feet high. Every hundred yards along the wall there was a turret occupied by a man. I didn't see any guns, but I was sure they were there. But the security measures didn't stop there. Around the wall, on the outside, there were soldiers stationed every few yards—Russian soldiers, not German.

I stopped to take a look, and almost immediately one of the soldiers yelled and waved me on. I walked on slowly, trying to look like a native out for a stroll and impressed by the big buildings.

When I reached the end of the park, I turned left and walked past the back of the hospital. Everything was the same as it had been on the other side, with Russian soldiers everywhere you looked. The place was guarded until it resembled the Kremlin. It was a cinch they weren't using all those soldiers just to guard Hermann Gruss. Whatever else they were doing there must be even more important than Oderbruch had hinted.

Walking into this place and making off with Gruss was going to be a little like strolling into the Tower of London and grabbing the royal jewels.

There was no chance to stop and really study the setup, but I got a good enough look in walking by to see how tough it would be. I walked on past and then cut back through the park, trying to think of something. I began to wish that I'd let the CIA send me back to Washington.

I walked over and caught the subway back to the center of the city. By the time I got there, my hangover was back plaguing me. I had a couple of drinks, which helped, but that is strictly the way to start building another one. It was the middle of the afternoon and I hadn't eaten yet. It wouldn't be long before the night shift would start at the Neva, so I decided I'd better attend to some food.

While I was eating, I struggled with my problem. Rather, my two problems, for I was also trying to think of some way to stay with Beate and Oderbruch without consuming so much liquor. If I was going to do anything about Gruss, I would need all my wits about me. What I needed was a handy little hangover remedy.

It struck me then. I hurried, finished my luncheon, and caught a taxi over to Oderbruch's office. I was lucky. He was in. The nurse said he'd see me in a minute.

While I waited, I dug out the medical journal I'd seen there the day before and read the second article more carefully. I'd been right about it. I had the solution to one of my problems and I might have part of the other answer.

The nurse motioned me to go in. I put the magazine down and went through the door.

"You're too early today, Lieutenant," Oderbruch said. He sounded brisk, but not unfriendly. "I still have to pay a visit to the hospital and I'll probably be a little late reaching the Neva tonight."

"That wasn't why I came," I said. "I've got a little problem which I thought you might help me solve."

"I'll be glad to help any way I can. What is it?"

"These parties every night are becoming a problem," I said. "I have a certain amount of work to do each day, but it's a little difficult after drinking so much. I don't see how you do it. Yesterday while I was waiting for you, I was reading a medical journal, as I think I told you. There was mention of some new wonder drug that will sober one up and relieve hangovers. It was called chlorproma-something."

"Chlorpromazine," he said with a smile. "As a matter of fact, it is excellent. I've used it myself, although I usually give myself an intravenous shot of vitamin B."

I made a face at the suggestion of a shot. "I think I'd prefer something that can be taken by mouth. Would you mind giving me a prescription for the drug? It's not dangerous, is it?"

"Not at all," he said. He pulled a prescription pad over to him. "How much do you think you'll need?"

"Enough to last about a week," I said. "By that time I should be finished with my assignment and won't need it. Although some of it might come in handy, the times when we are assigned to banquets."

He laughed. "Any doctor in Moscow should give it to you, if you explain what you want it for," he said. He scribbled on the pad and tore off the sheet. He waved it a few times to dry the ink and handed it to me. "There you are, Lieutenant. That ought to do the trick. I told you my experiments would have political importance."

"Saving the hangover of the MVD," I said. "By the way, Dr. Oderbruch, I've been thinking about your remarks last night concerning the political use of psychiatry. It is a most interesting concept. I'd like to know more about it. Have you written any other articles on the subject?"

He was obviously flattered. "Yes, I have," he said. "I've done a couple of pieces for *Socialist Science* published here in Berlin. You may not be familiar with the magazine in Russia."

"I am not," I admitted. "Would you have copies of the articles and would it be possible to borrow them? I can guarantee you that I will be most careful of them and will return them within a very few days."

As I suspected, flattery was the best weapon to use. "I do have copies of them," he said. "I'll be happy to lend them to you." He got up and went into an adjoining cubicle where there were file cabinets. He was out of sight in there, but I could hear him opening one of the drawers.

I reached over and quickly tore a dozen prescription sheets from the pad on his desk. I folded them in half and had them tucked away in my pocket by the time he returned with a couple of magazines. He handed them to me.

"The articles are really incomplete," he said in an attempt to be modest, "but you may find something of interest in them. When I've completed my present experiments, I expect to do a more thorough and serious piece on the subject."

"I'll be very interested to read these," I said. I stood up. "Thanks for the prescription. I expect I'll see you this evening."

"You certainly will," he said heartily. "Don't get too far ahead of me now that you've got a hangover remedy." He laughed.

I said good-bye and left. I went straight back to the Goethe Hotel. Rainer wasn't at the desk, but the man who was apparently knew of me. He told me I'd find Rainer down in the basement, toward the front. I went down the stairs and picked my way through boxes and barrels. Up ahead, I could see light streaming from an open doorway. I reached it and looked in. A small, comfortable room had been fixed up there. One wall was lined with books, old and worn from much handling. There was a chair and a couch. Rainer Hansske was stretched out on the couch, reading a book. He looked up and saw me standing in the doorway. He smiled.

"Exul ego clericus," he recited, *"ad laborem natus / tribulor multotiens / paupertati datus. / Literarum studiis / vellem insudare / nisi quod inopia / cogit me cessare."* He looked thoughtful. "Perhaps I should say the needs of my new profession rather than want."

"You lost me way back there," I said. "I recognize the Latin, but I never got beyond *amo, amas, amat.* The teacher was pretty and I couldn't see any point in saying 'All Gaul is divided into three parts' to her."

He chuckled. "I was merely repeating a rather ancient scholar's lament. Roughly, I was saying that I'm an exiled student, born to toil and thrown by poverty into many kinds of misery, and that I long to study my books but want compels me to stop. I suppose, however, in this case it is *your* want that compels me to stop. I gather from the look in your eye that you do want something."

"Have you got a good forger?" I asked.

"One of the best."

I pulled the prescription and the blanks from my pocket. "I want this prescription duplicated on each one of these blanks. The quicker I can get them the better."

He took them and glanced at them. "One hour," he said.

I nodded.

"Be right back," he said and left. I went over and looked at the books in the bookcase. He was back in less than ten minutes. "They'll be ready for you in an hour, maybe less."

"That didn't take long," I said. "Have you got the whole damn Berlin underground hidden away in this hotel?"

He chuckled. "Not quite. But Hans—he's the one who told you you could find me down here—used to be one of the best forgers in Germany. We were in Dachau together. Now his talents are mostly devoted to our needs. What are the prescriptions for?"

"It started out to be a cure for my hangover," I said, "but I think it's going to be part of the answer to getting Gruss out of East Germany."

He looked his question.

I dropped into the chair and lit a cigarette. "There are more damn theories on how Oderbruch got Gruss to come over than there are people in Berlin. The leading contender has been that Gruss had cancer and was convinced that only over here could he be cured. I began to get a different idea. Even Gruss's wife talked about cancer, but it seemed to me that what she was really afraid of was that her husband had a mental illness. Other little things I stumbled onto seemed to support that idea. Then yesterday I ran into something that proves it to me. You ever hear of lysergic acid diethylamide?"

He shook his head.

"It's a new drug that will produce all the symptoms of schizophrenia. Dr. Oderbruch is credited with doing a lot of experimental work with it. I think that Gruss is one of his experiments. I can see that to an imaginative man like Hermann Gruss the idea of having schizophrenia might be even more frightening than the thought of cancer."

"How could the doctor give him the drug without his suspecting something?" Rainer asked.

"I think that would have been easy with Gruss. He was a nervous, tense man to begin with. He thought Oderbruch was his friend; they'd been in the German underground together. He might complain to Oderbruch merely about feeling tense. Oderbruch could put on an act of thinking it might be more serious and give him something supposed to relieve the symptoms—actually lysergic acid diethylamide. Then, when Gruss called him or came to him in panic after the attack of schizophrenia was over, Oderbruch could tell him the worst. He might also tell him that he, Oderbruch, has been working on a cure. Over a period of time, he could prove that he was able to check or help the attacks. After that, it would be easy to get Gruss over to his special hospital. Almost any man, faced with insanity, would do what Gruss has done, even to trading bits of information in his hope of being cured."

"How would he convince Gruss he could cure it?"

"There is another drug that will check the symptoms. It would be even easier, since the symptoms were induced.

I imagine that even when Gruss made the trip to America, Oderbruch controlled it by giving Gruss two kinds of medicine to take. One if he felt nervous—that was the one to bring on an attack. The other was to take when an attack occurred, and would stop the attack. I was told that Gruss was sick while in America and wouldn't see an American doctor. He had medicine with him."

"Yes," Rainer said, nodding, "I can see where that might work—especially with an imaginative man. It is the antidote which is called for by the prescriptions Hans is forging?"

"Yes. If I reach Gruss, I can use it to convince him of what has been happening. Once I've done that, he should be more than willing to go back with me. All this, of course, providing my intuition isn't haywire. Incidentally, Oderbruch told me that he was a double agent when Hitler was in power and that it was he who tipped off the Nazi Party to the bomb plot against Hitler."

"When you've rescued Gruss," Rainer said, "would you like to leave Oderbruch to the care of the underground?"

"I want to take him back, too. He'll be worth more to us alive than dead."

"I suppose so," the old man said with a sigh. "You know where Gruss is?"

I nodded. "You know the New Lenin Hospital out at Schloss Park?"

"Yes. We've never been able to find out much about it, but the story was that it was a Red Army hospital and that Russians were being brought there for some kind of treatment. The only arrivals have always come late at night in closed cars. Is that where Gruss is held?"

"Yes. Oderbruch is carrying out other experiments there, too. He didn't even give a hint as to what they are, but I have an idea that knowing what they are might be even more important than rescuing Gruss."

"You have a plan for getting in the hospital?"

"No," I admitted. "And it's going to take some doing. The place is surrounded by Russian soldiers. Got any ideas?"

"We could perhaps organize some sort of workers' riot and have the men attack the hospital," he said.

I shook my head. "It would be a massacre. I'm not sure it would work anyway, and I certainly don't want to sacrifice a lot of lives. Force won't do it, not with anything less than a well-equipped regiment of soldiers."

"Maybe we could go out at night, knock off a couple of guards, or distract them in some way, giving you a chance to go over the wall."

I shook my head again. "I don't want to risk any of the underground here. Every one of you is valuable. In the meantime, I have only one hint of an idea and I'm not sure it'll work. I noticed all the guards on the outside were Red Army men. Do you know if the MVD have any men there?"

"They do," he said. "I don't know how many, but there are some stationed inside. I think they're changed every two or three days. We could find out for you by tomorrow."

"Too late," I said. "If I want to give myself any margin of safety at all, I've got to try to get Gruss out by tomorrow night."

"That's a big order."

"I know, but I don't have any choice." I told him what had happened with Kuibykov and the MVD colonel.

"Maybe you should give it up," he suggested, "and let them send someone else in."

"I'm a stubborn man," I said. "I'm not going back without at least trying."

"I make it a policy never to argue with a stubborn man. What is your plan?"

"It's not really a plan; it's an act of desperation," I said. "I told the MVD colonel that I was here to check up on Oderbruch. So I'm going to ask him to get me into the hospital as one of his men. It may work. If it does, I'll be in there with Gruss and I'll play it by ear after that."

He nodded. "It might work at that. I've noticed that sometimes boldness will produce results where everything else fails. If you do not return by tomorrow night, you want us to try to get you out?"

"No. And that's a definite order. No one in the East Berlin underground is to be risked more than he already has been. There's just one thing that might be done. If the Colonel falls for my suggestion, I'll be back here to get my things. But something might go wrong at the beginning. If I'm not back here by tomorrow morning, phone Horst Henckels' café in West Berlin and leave a message for Henri Flambeau. The message is that the young man of Provence is somewhat smaller than he was."

"The young man of Provence is somewhat smaller than he was," he repeated. He thought a minute and smiled. "It is from a French limerick, is it not? I seem to remember."

"That's right," I said. I recited the whole limerick for him and he nodded, grinning with memory. "You know," I went on, "I've often thought of suggesting to the United Nations that a liking for limericks might be the test for those people who are being considered for a one-world setup."

"That would rule out the Communists," he said. "They have no sense of humor."

"Maybe they would like limericks," I suggested, "if they were written with more political content. Something on the order of ... There was a young capitalist from Mott, whom a passion for money besot." I stopped, trying to think how the rest of it might go.

"Till he discovered Karl Marx, was made Commissar of Parks," Rainer supplied.

"And became dialectically hot," I finished. We both laughed at our little collaboration. "Maybe," I said, "I should submit it to Herr Schwabach for consideration of the Central Committee."

"They'd probably study it very seriously," he said. "They'd appoint a subcommittee to bring in a report and, after due deliberation, they'd reject it for the new agitprop campaign on the basis of a suspicion of Trotskyite leanings."

"Then I guess we'll just have to let them go unlearned."

"They are unlearned," he said seriously. "And so are those who submitted to them. If they were not, they too would have asked who would protect the many against the many."

"Another quotation?" I asked.

He nodded. "Goethe was thinking about the French Revolution when he asked the question, but it applies now. Do you know the passage?"

Frankreichs traurig Geschick, die Grossen mögen's bedenken
Aber bedenken fürwahr sollen es Kleine noch mehr.
Grosse gingen zu Grunde: doch wer beschützte die Menge
Gegen die Menge? Da war Menge der Menge Tyrann.*

He was silent for a minute and then said:

Alle Freiheits-Apostel, sie waren mir immer zuwider;
Willkür suchte doch nur Jeder am ende für sich.**

"The Apostles of Freedom seek nothing but license," I repeated. "You know, you're starting to convince me that Goethe was talking about the present."

"He was talking about now and for all times. But don't think this applies only to the Communists. The Communists are trying to crush all men and form them into soulless automatons who will exist in collective insecurity. But what answer does America, Great Britain, France, and even India have? Only to form a more perfect mass man to overpower Russia's mass man. This, my friend, is a battle which does not end with either the East or the West winning. The real war is between Mass Man and Individual Man. And who will speak for us? The last great spokesman for Individual Man died with Gandhi."

"I'm inclined to agree with you," I said, "but the question is, what are any of us doing about it? What will we do about it?"

---

* From *Venetian Epigrams* (1789): "The sad fate of France, the great may ponder it, but the small in truth still more. Great ones went to their ruin; but who protects the crowd from the crowd? The crowd becomes the crowd's tyrant."
** "All apostles of freedom were always revolting to me; each in the end seeks license for himself alone."

He laughed bitterly. "I will tell you a story which gives you the answer. A Frenchman, an Englishman, an American, and a German were asked to give a report on the elephant. The Frenchman rushed to the Jardin des Plantes, spent an hour in research, returned, and wrote a *feuilleton* which the Academy found faultless, but which added nothing to our knowledge of the elephant.

"The Englishman went to Africa, hired a competent white hunter, and spent two years studying the elephant. He then returned home and spent another three years writing a huge book filled with facts, but devoid of order or philosophy.

"The American hired a poll-taker to make an exhaustive survey of elephants. When it was completed, he had an efficiency expert go over it, after which he went into the business of breeding and selling elephants. And he hired a publicity man to convince the whole world that elephants were necessary to their continued existence.

"The German had nothing but contempt for the frivolity of the Frenchman, the lack of philosophy in the Englishman, and the crude opportunism of the American. He retired to his study and began to work on something which he called 'The Idea of the Elephant and Its Relationship to Moral Consciousness.' He is still working on it."

I laughed. "You should have included a Russian. He would have written an article called 'The Elephant and the Five-Year Plan,' then rushed out to organize the elephants into the working class."

He grinned back happily. "In the meantime, planting as many agents as possible among the white hunters and ivory collectors just in case there's a change in the Party Line." He glanced at his watch. "Your prescriptions should be ready by now. I will bring them."

He was back in less than ten minutes with the prescriptions in his hand. He looked at them, shaking his head. "Hans does a good job," he said admiringly. "The doctor himself couldn't tell which he wrote and which Hans did. It must be true, as he claims, that he's the best forger in Europe."

I took the prescriptions and looked at them. They were good. I'd had some experience with forgery and I couldn't spot a thing in them. "He's good," I admitted. "What do you find for him to do?"

"We keep a fairly steady stream of false orders floating about East Germany. It adds to the confusion. Then there are special jobs like this one. But we don't keep him too busy. I think he carries on a rather healthy side line of his own in ration cards and East German marks. It keeps his hand in and adds to the troubles of the Communists. We in the underground here encourage individual initiative as long as it doesn't endanger what we're working for. Hans is also invaluable in that he resembles Goethe's Nature."

I stood up. "I'll let you educate me in regard to the similarity between Nature and a spy, and then I must go."

"Und was sie deinem Geist nicht offenbaren mag, das zwingst du ihr nicht ab mit Hebeln und mit Schrauben," he said. "And what she does not reveal to the mind will not be extorted from her by levers and screws."

"You've almost convinced me I should reread Goethe if I ever get out of here," I said. "Much better than Mickey Spillane. In the meantime, Rainer, it's been nice knowing you. If I don't see you again, give Hedwig a pat on the bottom for me and take care of yourself." I held out my hand.

He reached and shook my hand warmly. "Thank you, Milo," he said. "If you'll pardon another reference, you have helped to make this earthly ball a peopled garden for me. You are sure there is nothing you will let me do to help you?"

"Nothing more than the message," I said firmly. "This is an operation that needs a couple thousand men or one man. Anything in between would only be unwieldy."

"All right," he said. He was still holding my hand. "In the old days, I would have said, 'Go with God.' But now, with both my life and Dachau behind me, I say go with luck, my friend."

"Thanks, Rainer," I said. "If I don't get back, I'll see you in *das Land wo die Zitronen blühn.*"

"Im dunkeln Laub die Gold-Orangen glühn," he said softly.

I left him there, thinking of Goethe and good-bye, and went swiftly up the stairs and through the lobby to the street. I had grown rather fond of Rainer Hansske the few days I'd known him, and I hated to leave him almost as badly as he hated to see me go. In my opinion, there wasn't very much of anything good in Germany, but what there was could be found in him.

It took me the better part of an hour to fill all the prescriptions, handing in only one at each drugstore. By the end of that time, I had about three hundred little orange tablets. It was then fairly late in the afternoon. I'd have to work fast if I wanted to do any more before evening. And I wanted to. I was afraid to leave it over to the next day because my time would be cut down that much more.

I retired to the nearest café and had a drink while I thought the whole thing over. The only idea I had was the one of going to see Colonel Nadashev of the MVD. I'd already told him that I was here to investigate Oderbruch. Now I'd try asking for his help to get inside Oderbruch's hospital. It was strictly a long shot, but it was also my best bet for a fast entrance. I had a feeling that the Colonel might play along. As for getting out after I found Gruss, I'd have to play that the way it fell.

Which left me with another problem. Three hundred pills of chlorpromazine. The pills were small, but even so, three hundred made a fair-sized bunch. I needed those for Gruss— and I might need them for myself if I were caught. And in the latter case, I had to have them where they wouldn't be found when I was searched, even though the first search probably wouldn't be too thorough. I knew one trick that a lot of diamond and drug smugglers use, and for a minute I did think of trying to get a long, thin tube. But three hundred pills laid end to end would be enough to give me a tonsillec-tomy—from the wrong end.

I finally went out and browsed around in the small shops in the neighborhood until I found what I wanted. A little cotton bag that would hold the pills, yet was still much smaller than my fist. I bought some adhesive tape. Then I went into a men's room, filled the bag with the pills, and taped the whole right up in the fork between my legs. If they caught me, they wouldn't be apt to be looking to see if I had a hernia, and it ought to escape any other examination.

Now I was about as ready as I'd ever be. I went back into the café and had a double brandy just on the chance that it might be my last chance. Then I headed for Unter den Linden and the headquarters of the MVD.

It was late when I arrived there, but still well within the working day. The same uniformed young man was at the desk in the outer office. When he finally consented to look up, I saluted him.

"Lieutenant Nalyevo," I said, "requesting an official interview with Colonel Nadashev."

There was a phone on his desk, but he got up and disappeared through the door back of his desk. He was gone only a minute.

"Colonel Nadashev will see you soon," he said and went back to reading the magazine before him on the desk. By twisting my neck, I could see that it was one of the popular Russian magazines rather than a political one. I sat and waited.

Probably fifteen minutes passed before there was any action. Then the phone on the young man's desk burred softly. He picked up the receiver and listened. He replaced the receiver without saying anything and nodded at me.

"Go in," he said.

I walked over, opened the door, and stepped into the office. The Colonel was seated behind his desk. I saluted him. After he returned the salute, he stood up and held out his hand. It seemed like a good beginning.

"Lieutenant Nalyevo," he said, "it is nice to see you so soon again. I apologize for making you wait so long."

"It was nothing," I said. I sat down in the chair beside his desk.

"You are still seeing Frau Schwabach?" he asked. "Then perhaps you would appreciate a little vodka?"

I nodded.

He pulled the bottle and glasses from his desk and poured the drinks. He sighed.

"Ah, to be young. I well remember in my younger days, there were many Frau Schwabachs. It is pleasant." He handed me a glass.

"Za vashe zdorovye," I said, lifting my glass.

He lifted his and then we drank.

"Ah, there is nothing like our own vodka," he said. "I tell you frankly, Lieutenant, I never had any trouble getting used to foreign women, but I've never been able to drink their liquor."

"I prefer our own," I said, "but I confess if none is available I can drink the other."

He nodded. "When you're young, you can drink anything. But I am sure, Lieutenant, that you did not drop around just to hear my views on women and vodka. What can I do for you?"

"I need some help," I said. "I think I told you that my assignment is to check up on Dr. Oderbruch."

He nodded again. "Ah, yes, Dr. Oderbruch. Apparently a good man—but still not a Russian."

"Exactly, Colonel. But I've run into a slight obstacle. In order to make my report complete, I must get in this hospital of his—which he thoughtfully named the New Lenin—and I must do it without revealing myself to him. I'm aware that you have men stationed inside there, and I thought perhaps you could put me in as one of your men. Just for a day or two, of course."

He swung around and stared out the window. I remembered the gesture from the other day.

"It could be done," he said. "When would you like to go to the hospital?"

"Tonight, if possible," I said. "The quicker I can complete my investigation, the quicker I will be able to take my report back."

He swung back and stared at me with a little smile playing around his lips. "The young are always in a hurry," he said. "But I suppose that is good. You know, in a way, I am sorry that you didn't come to me with this request yesterday."

"Why?"

"Yesterday," he said, "within an hour, within half an hour, I would have had you at the hospital replacing one of my men. I liked you when you came to see me the other day and wished that you had been assigned to me. I still wish it. But today I have no choice but to tell you that I must place you under arrest—Major Milo March."

EIGHT

He caught me when I was least expecting it with that last sentence. He had led up to it with a sense of timing that was rare in Russians, and I could tell by the expression on his face that he was enjoying it. He could afford to. There were only two ways out of the room. One was the window and a three-floor drop, but he could probably reach it before I could. The other was the door, but it was a safe bet that there were any number of husky MVD men standing out there and waiting for me to try it. The only thing I could do was roll with the punch and wait for an opening.

"Well," I said lightly, "that's the way it goes. One day chicken and the next day feathers—mixed with a little tar."

He laughed. "I like you, Major March. You know, I was quite serious when I said that I wished you were one of my men. It is a pleasure to meet an agent of your caliber. Most of those who come are stupid. But you speak Russian like a native and you are clever. Only a very clever agent would have dared come into East Berlin within two hours of having been exposed."

"I would be more flattered," I said, "if I didn't know that I was going to have to pay for every one of those compliments. May I smoke, Colonel?"

"Of course," he said. "Would you care for another vodka?"

I nodded, getting out a cigarette and lighting it. He poured two more drinks and pushed one across to me.

"To your health," he said.

"To my health," I agreed. We drank.

"You know, Major," he said, putting his glass down, "I am almost sorry that you are caught, although it would have gone badly for me if you weren't. This is a most serious matter. You are an American Army officer caught inside East Germany in a Russian uniform. There is no escaping the conclusions and the results."

"It seems that way."

"You do not fully agree?" he said. "Good. I can't stand men who give up easily. You would have disappointed me if you had done so." Without asking me, he poured two more drinks.

"Mind telling me how it happened?" I asked.

"Not at all. Officially, you understand, I will take full credit for uncovering a master spy. But it really was a stroke of luck. It seems that our Dr. Oderbruch became worried last night because he felt he might have talked too much to you. He was still worrying about it when you came to him today, requesting a prescription of a drug he's been experimenting with and also wanting to know more about his work. Dr. Oderbruch is a suspicious man—he once demanded an investigation of me, so don't feel that you made a mistake. While you were in his office, he noticed you lean your hand on his desk. As soon as you were gone, he had us over to take your fingerprints from the desk and to hear his suspicions."

"I underestimated the good doctor," I said.

"But it was not cleverness," he said. "Only fear. After the

experience with Kuibykov and having met you and liked you, I put very little stock in the doctor's tale. Still, we went through the gestures just to quiet the doctor. You may imagine my surprise—although I concealed it from everyone—when your fingerprints matched those of Major Milo March of the American Army. I at once telephoned Moscow, determined that there was no Lieutenant Nalyevo, and informed them that, through my own cleverness, Major March would soon be in my custody."

"Sounds as if you're making a big deal out of it."

"Now you underestimate yourself," he said reproachfully. "You are a famous man in East Germany and in Russia, Major. It is only two years since you came into East Germany and kidnapped a valuable Western deserter. We have remembered it well. In fact, my predecessor owes his present assignment in Siberia to that visit of yours."

"That's how you happened to have my fingerprints?"

"Oh, yes. They were taken when you were briefly arrested that time. Since then, your prints have been within easy reach of every MVD office. You may be interested to know that I was opposed to the publicity about your present trip. I would have preferred letting you come and then grabbing you, but it was ordered from someone higher."

"You didn't know I was still coming?"

"No," he admitted. "We were sure an agent had been sent in replacing you, and I confess that for a moment it crossed my mind that a man as clever as yourself might have come ahead with a different identity, but then I dismissed it. We knew, of course, that someone had come, because a member of the German Secret Police was killed in the subway. He would have been following anyone who came in." His eyes widened with surprise. "I have just remembered. The report on Willi Borm's death mentioned that in running away, the killer collided with an unidentified MVD officer. It was you, was it not? You killed him, ran to the stairway, and doubled back?"

"Something like that. Although Willi Borm was killed accidentally."

He waved a hand. "It makes no difference. He was not important."

"Tell me one thing," I said casually. "Who tipped you off to my coming in the first place?"

He gave me a big smile. "No, no, Major. It might seem safe with you under arrest, but you are a clever man and you are not yet executed. Perhaps I might whisper it to you when you finally face the firing squad, but even then I am not sure."

"Okay," I said. "Bring on the chains and the dungeons."

"Oh, nothing like that," he said. "In fact, you are going to get your request granted."

"What does that mean?"

"You are being sent to New Lenin Hospital."

"As one of Oderbruch's guinea pigs?" I asked.

"In a way," he said. "You are important enough, Major March, to warrant a full treatment. Public trial and all that. Dr. Oderbruch has convinced Moscow that he has special talents to be used in such cases. So you are to be turned over to him to be prepared for the trial."

I was interested and amused, and at the same time, I suppose, a little apprehensive. I was interested because if I was sent to the hospital, I'd probably get a chance to see Gruss or at least find out something about him. My feeling also was that there would be a better chance of breaking out of the hospital, despite its heavy guard, than from a prison. I was amused because I knew it meant Oderbruch thought he could make me confess. And a little apprehensive because if my guess was right, he was experimenting with man-made schizophrenia. A business of now-you're-insane, now-you're-sane might be hard to take.

"Oderbruch's going to make me confess?" I asked.

"I think he regards you as a challenge," the Colonel said. "The report on you includes the questioning you went through when you were arrested in East Germany before."

"The doctor is ambitious," I couldn't help saying.

He shook his head. "I tell you, Major March, that I went through and survived the purge in Russia twenty years ago, but I would not want to be turned over to the doctor's gentle care. I will also tell you, just between the two of us, that I do not think that brave men such as yourself should be subjected to such things. Shot, yes—that is part of the game, accepted as such—but these things, no."

"Thanks," I said. I didn't bother telling him that I preferred it this way; there's something so final about being shot.

"Another vodka before you go?" the Colonel asked.

"No, thanks," I said. "I don't want to take advantage of your hospitality."

"It was the least I could do for a brave and clever man,"

he said. He put the bottle and glasses away with a seeming reluctance; "I shall probably not see you again, Major March, unless it should be at your trial. I have enjoyed our two brief talks and I shall regret that we will not be able to have more of them."

"So will I," I said, grinning. "I'll tell you what I'll do, Colonel. When I get back to New York, I'll send a postcard. With the Statue of Liberty on it."

He grinned back at me. "I admire your spirit, Major, but it is useless. Some of my best men will be stationed inside the hospital, and there is a regiment of the Red Army surrounding the outside."

"I know," I said. "I'll still send you that postcard." I didn't feel as confident as I sounded, but I'd be damned if I'd let him know it.

He shrugged, reaching out to press a button in the base of his phone. The door opened and two big MVD men stepped into the room and saluted. Through the open door I could see two more.

"This is Major Milo March," he told them. "He is to be delivered to Dr. Oderbruch at New Lenin Hospital. Major March is a brave and clever agent. I suggest that you exercise caution."

"Yes, sir," said one of the men. He turned to me and ordered me to come with them, switching to a crude German.

"Major March," the Colonel said dryly, "speaks Russian better than you do. In the meantime, I suggest that you start exercising caution by searching Major March before taking him out."

The man looked startled. He turned and ran his hands roughly over me, looking for a gun or a knife. He took my identity card, some meaningless papers, my cigarettes, and all my money from my pockets. He looked at the Colonel.

"Give him back his cigarettes," the Colonel ordered. "Turn the other things over to the captain in charge at the hospital." He glanced at me. "You were going into this unarmed, Major?"

"Armed only with my wits," I said lightly. "As it's turned out, it seems that I was weaponless."

For the first time he looked at me with a worried look on his face. "Strange," he said. "You are a brave man. There is no question about that. But you are taking this much more calmly than I expected." He brooded on it for a minute, then waved to his men. "Well, take him away. Be careful. They will search him more thoroughly at the hospital."

The two men marched me out of his office. The other two fell in as we reached the foyer. All four of them stayed close around me as we went downstairs. A number of people looked at us curiously and then looked as hurriedly away. They knew it was an arrest and it seemed to inspire fear in all of them. Down on the street, two of the men walked on either side of me, the third directly in front and the fourth right behind me. That's the way it stayed until we reached a big Zis sedan with official plates on it.

They put me in the back seat between two of the men. The other two got in the front, but the one that wasn't driving twisted around until he was facing me. The Colonel's suggestion to be careful was being taken seriously. I began to feel like the Willie Sutton of the political world.*

We drove out Unter den Linden to König and then onto Frankfurter, which led into Allee Alt-Friedrichsfelde. We stayed on that until we hit Treskow Allee. A few minutes later, the car pulled up in front of the hospital.

The soldiers at the main entrance examined the papers of my guards as if they expected to find a spy in the wrinkles. They looked me over just as carefully. Finally, they opened the gates and we drove inside the walls.

They parked the car in front of the building. At the door we had another halt while more men, this time MVD, examined my guards' papers and asked questions about me. When they were finally satisfied, my four guards turned me over to two husky substitutes. They marched me down the long, gleaming white corridor. Once, as we passed a row of windows, I saw a number of men walking aimlessly around on the grounds outside. They looked as if they might be inmates.

"Steady customers?" I asked my escorts.

They ignored me.

We marched almost to the end of the corridor and then took an elevator to the fourth floor. Then we went back along the corridor. There were doors all along it, all of them closed. This looked more like the straitjacket section of the hospital.

We finally arrived at a room where they turned me over to two men wearing white coats. They were dressed like doctors, but they looked more like bouncers.

---

* Willie Sutton was a notorious bank robber of the 1930s to '50s who escaped prison several times.

"Undress," one of them said to me in Russian as soon as the two guards left.

"I don't think we've been introduced," I said, "and my mother told me never to undress in front of strange men."

"Very amusing," he said. He stared at me stolidly. "Get undressed."

It seemed to be a losing argument, so I got undressed. He stopped me when I'd stripped down to my shorts. I was glad. I knew that any really thorough physical examination would quickly turn up my cache of pills.

Then the two of them went over me with a stethoscope, grunting back and forth to each other without saying anything. They looked in my eyes, ears, nose, and mouth. They prodded at my neck, chest, and stomach. At last they seemed to be in agreement on the whole thing.

"Come on," one of them said.

I started to pick up my clothes. "Leave them there," he said. "You won't be needing them. Come on."

They led me out into the corridor and two rooms farther along. They opened the door and ushered me into a large room. It was well lighted. In the center there was a large table with four comfortable chairs around it. On one side there was a plain single bed. There were four men seated at the table, with pads of paper and pencils in front of three of them. The fourth man was Dr. Franz Oderbruch.

"He's in perfect health," one of the men with me reported.

"Good," Oderbruch said crisply. He waited until the two men had left and then turned his attention to me. "Stand there," he said, indicating a spot about two feet from where I was standing.

"I like it here," I said. I watched his face tighten with anger. "Aren't you going to introduce me to your friends?" He obviously wasn't.

"Tell me, Doctor," I went on, "aren't you a little bit worried about working so late? With you and me both away, Kuibykov is going to be making time with Beate."

"It makes no difference," he said coldly. "The combination of my work and having caught you will make it unnecessary for me to need any sponsorship here."

I laughed to myself. Maybe his work would do it, but he certainly wasn't going to get any credit for catching me. Official sources wouldn't even know he had anything to do with it.

Oderbruch turned to the other men at the table. "This," he said, "is Major Milo March, an American spy whom I was instrumental in apprehending this afternoon. He was sent here to try to kidnap Herr Gruss, about whom you have already heard me talk."

"Good evening, gentlemen," I said gravely. "Herr Doktor Oderbruch has made one slight mistake. I am Lieutenant Nalyevo, of the Russian MVD."

"The identity he adopted for his spying," Oderbruch said. "At this point, you will notice, he refuses even to concede his real identity. This is good. It will make my experiment that much more startling. Actually, of course, the full process which will guarantee his behavior at a trial will take a few weeks, but I think I can promise you some rather startling changes even in a week."

"The Oderbruch formula of brainwashing?" I asked.

"Something like that," he admitted calmly. "Now, Major March, I intend to give you a small quantity of a drug. You may have it in a glass of water, if you like, which will be tasteless. Or, if you insist on being stubborn, I will merely call in attendants and have them hold you while I give it to you intravenously. Which do you prefer?"

"What is it?" I asked. "Lysergic acid diethylamide?"

"Exactly. Which method do you prefer?"

There wasn't much point in arguing about it. I knew that they could certainly produce enough men to hold me while he gave me an injection. Besides, I had the antidote and something might happen to it in any struggle.

"I'll drink it," I said.

"Good. I'm glad that you're going to be sensible." He walked in back of the table and got a pitcher of water and a glass. He poured water into the glass. He took a small metal case from his pocket and extracted from it an eyedropper. At first, I thought it was empty, but I finally realized there was liquid in it, such a small amount as to be almost invisible.

"This, gentlemen," he said, "is lysergic acid diethylamide. Fifty micrograms, fifty millionths of a gram, to be exact. As you can see, it is such a small amount as to be almost invisible. Yet this is a large enough dose to put the patient into a schizophrenic state for seven to eight hours."

I began to be glad I had the antidote with me.

Oderbruch held the eyedropper over the glass of water and squeezed the bulb. The infinitesimal drop of liquid slid into the water and vanished. He stepped around the table and handed the glass to me.

"Drink it," he said, "and then go over and lie on the couch until you begin to feel something."

Even with the risk, I was tempted to throw the glass in his face, but I knew that would only bring the attendants. It would be better to play along. Maybe my chance would come.

I lifted the glass and tasted the water. It tasted like ordinary water. I drank it down and handed the glass back to him. Then I walked over to the couch and stretched out.

"You gentlemen," Oderbruch said, "will now have the opportunity to see how the drug works. As I said, he will be in the state for seven or eight hours and we can watch as much of that time as you wish."

I didn't get it right away, but when I did, it hit me like a ton of bricks. I'd been thinking that Oderbruch would slip me the dose, and they'd lead me into a room with padded walls and leave me there. Then I'd take the antidote and everything would be all right. Now I realized they weren't going to do anything of the kind. They were going to sit right there and watch me, and I'd have no chance to take the antidote at all.

For the first time in my life, I think, I suddenly knew real fear. It bit deep into my stomach, twisting my bowels until there was physical pain. It numbed my brain, driving out all thoughts but one—that I was a prisoner inside of a body that would soon be possessed by drugs.

I don't know how long the fear lasted, but I fought it silently within myself, and after a bit it subsided. Oh, I was still afraid of being insane, but it was no longer the torturing thing it had been. I don't suppose man is capable of feeling no fear about insanity—even temporary insanity. We are all of us pretty superstitious and primitive about madness, and until we can wipe out the last vestige of that, there will be fear and awe of insanity. But I had fought it down to where it was more rational.

Other men, I told myself, had gone into the depths of schizophrenia, many to spend a lifetime there, others merely to visit it under the influence of the drug that was now in me. They had survived. Gruss, too—and I was now sure that was what had happened to him—had undoubtedly survived doses of this drug several times and he was still around. Not only still around, but quite obviously still withholding some information.

I began to feel better and to realize that the four men were deep in a discussion of the drug I'd been given. I couldn't remember them starting the discussion, so they had probably been at it some time.

"Almost twenty minutes," I heard Oderbruch say. "I shouldn't be long now."

I knew he was referring to me and when the drug would start working. I lay there, every muscle rigid, waiting for the madness to start creeping into my brain, not knowing what form it would take. Could I even fight it, I wondered. I was determined to, even though I didn't know how to begin. I'd gone through a number of pretty bad beatings in my time, and once two years before I'd gone through a marathon questioning at the hands of the Communists. In those cases, too, there had been no way to stop what was being done to me, but I'd managed somehow to escape within myself so that the pain was bearable. But how did you escape from your own brain?

I was aware that the room had grown colder. I could feel it

in my legs and feet. I sat up on the bed and stamped my feet on the floor. "Why don't you get a little heat in here, Oderbruch?" I asked. "My feet are cold."

"Note the time, gentlemen," Oderbruch said. His voice sounded odd, as though there were on echo in the room. "It is just twenty-three minutes since he took the drug. Coldness in the lower extremities is always the first symptom."

I realized what he was saying, and for a minute the panic threatened to run through me again, but I fought if off. Then I forgot it as I waited, almost holding my breath, for whatever might be the next symptom.

My legs were trembling slightly. I couldn't tell whether it was from the cold or was the next step. It was enough to make me feel like lying down, but I resisted. Somehow, I felt I'd be better able to meet whatever was coming if I was upright.

"If you'll notice carefully," Oderbruch's voice floated across the room, "you will see a slight tremor in his knees. This usually comes immediately after the coldness."

I stared at him for a full minute before I realized that again he was talking about me, discussing me as coldly as if I'd been a cadaver placed there. I began to get angry about it. I stared at him harder. It seemed to me that his face had taken on a long, droopy look. Maybe it was the light or maybe he'd always looked that way and I was seeing him as he really was, for the first time. A long, droopy face like a baboon. Or a gibbering gibbon. Was there such a thing as a gibbon? I wasn't sure.

But I was sure of my anger.

"You son of a bitch," I said to him. "You sit there staring at me and you don't even look like a human."

"Thirty-one minutes after taking the drug," Oderbruch said. "You will note the emotional flatness and the distorted vision."

All right, I thought, if he's going to treat me like a lab specimen, I won't say another damn word. Not a single double-damn word. I sat there, ignoring them, trying to concentrate on how I felt. There wasn't anything special. I felt a little peculiar, but no more so than at times when I'd been drunk. The big changes must come later on. Later on …

I didn't know how much later on it was. I knew I'd been sitting there, determined to do something, but I couldn't remember what it was. And suddenly I had an idea. Right out of left field.

"I just thought of something," I told Oderbruch. "I'll bet this whole thing is a fake. I'll bet you're a fake. You give everyone plain water and try to suggest that they're going insane. You were always interested in hypnotism. And that's what you're doing now."

"You saw the drug dropped in, Major March," Oderbruch said.

"I saw something dropped in, but it could've been just more water. Or maybe the drug company tricked you."

"That is impossible," he said.

"You don't have to shout," I said. "I can hear you. Too damn well. And see you too damn well, too. All four of you sitting around that table like a bunch of damned gargoyles. The ugliest bunch of bastards I ever saw."

"Fifty minutes since the drug was administered," Oderbruch intoned. "There is now a general feeling of suspiciousness and of persecution. Distortion of vision is now constant."

I made a loud suggestion about what he could go and do to himself. He didn't make any observation about that. The four of them just sat there, staring at me. And all four of them looked like something made by a guy named Frankenstein.

I decided not to talk to them anymore. To hell with them. I wouldn't talk to them and I wouldn't look at them. There were more pleasant things to look at. Even the bare walls of the room.

Funny. I'd thought it was a much larger room. I glanced from wall to wall, trying to guess the exact size of the room. I thought I had it once, but when I glanced again to check on it, I realized that the room was much smaller than my estimate. Then I suddenly realized what was happening. Oderbruch had some way of controlling the walls of the room with a switch. He was making the walls move in so that the room would get smaller.

No, it was worse than that. He was moving all the walls in so that within a few minutes they'd crush me. Well, anyway, that was something I could understand. I'd been through that kind of ordeal before. He wouldn't get anything out of me.

I gritted my teeth and waited, watching the walls come closer and closer. And still closer.

Four walls coming together.

I could feel my breath whistle out between my teeth. Somebody in the room screamed, but I was sure it wasn't me.

The walls were back in their regular places. Oderbruch had chickened out at the last minute and withdrawn them. That would show him. By now he knew I wasn't going to be so easy to break; he couldn't scare me with such childish tricks. I'd seen Harry Blackstone do better ones than that.*

"...well into the schizophrenic phase," Oderbruch was saying. "The rest of the phase will be marked by morbid feelings breaking like waves over the mind."

What the hell was he talking about now? He was always running off at the mouth about something. A blabbermouth.

"Blabbermouth," I said.

I was going to say something else, but I forgot it as I looked down at the floor. I couldn't see my own feet. They had to be there—I thought I could feel them—but I couldn't see them. I wiggled my toes, but I couldn't see any motion. Then I realized why. I was wearing shoes. So I waved the whole foot. Nothing. I tried pounding both feet on the floor. I heard a noise, all right—but it was probably Oderbruch trying to fool me, for I still couldn't see anything.

"Feet," I said.

"What about your feet, Major March?" Oderbruch asked.

"Feet," I said. "I had them when I came in."

That sounded pretty funny, I realized. So funny that I might have laughed, but not having any feet wasn't a laughing matter. If anything it was a crying matter. I felt as if I wanted to cry. But I didn't want them to see me. I closed my eyes so that I could cry behind the lids. That would fool them.

The colors were beautiful. Great arcing streamers of color, shooting up in front of my closed eyes and bursting into brighter colors. Like the fireworks on the Fourth of July. Only

---

* Harry Blackstone, Sr., was a well-known stage magician and illusionist.

prettier. I opened my eyes and they were gone. But my feet were back. It looked like a pretty good trade.

"Two hours and five minutes since the drug was administered," Oderbruch was saying, although his voice sounded a little like Beate's.

I didn't say anything. But I thought. Two hours and five minutes. Were the two hours married? Or maybe the five minutes wasn't theirs. I had to do something, if only the four gargoyles would stop watching me. It was terribly important.

"Major March."

I had to do it, but for the minute I couldn't think what it was. Something to do with taking something. For something.

"Major March."

"You don't have to shout, you son of a bitch," I said. "I'm not deaf."

"How do you feel now?" he asked.

"How do you expect me to feel?" I said. I watched my left arm raise up in the air and the fingers wiggle. "How would you feel if your actions weren't your own?"

"What do you mean, your actions aren't your own?"

"What I said. Everything I seem to be doing, somebody else is doing it. Some son of a bitch is doing it."

"Who?"

"Son of a bitch," I said. I knew who the son of a bitch was and I was going to tell him, but I was interrupted. The damnedest thing was happening. I was starting to float up toward the ceiling—but my body was still down on the bed. At first, I thought it was a trick. A funny trick. I giggled.

But it wasn't. I was really floating away from my body, and

how would I ever manage to get back to it? I tried swimming through the air, but my arms were back down there on my body. I was going to be lost out in space forever. If I didn't have my body, nobody could see me and they'd never be able to find me.

Somebody screamed in the room again, and then I was back in my body. I wondered who had screamed.

I sat staring at the floor. It was the strangest floor I'd ever seen. It moved, undulating back and forth like a carpet of snakes. A carpet of red and yellow snakes. Only they moved in rhythm. I could feel it under my feet.

The carpet moved and slithered and wriggled. It coiled around my legs, creeping upward. Somebody in the room screamed.

"Three hours and fifty minutes." The voice was loud and booming.

My voice hurt from the screaming. I was doing the screaming, but I wasn't. It was a me that had nothing to do with me. A me away from me.

A home away from home. A me away from me. A scream without a screamer. I stared at the floor again because maybe if I looked hard enough I'd see what was happening to me.

"What are you thinking about, Major March?"

"I sit here looking so absorbed," I said. It was my voice, but I wasn't using it. "I cannot see that I am absorbed in anything but nothing."

I opened my mouth but no sound came out. A screamer without a scream.

I giggled.

Somewhere there had to be a scream. Oderbruch pressed a button and somebody screamed with my voice. I knew him for what he was. I hated him for what I was. I knew there was something he was, but I couldn't say it. A lazy obscenity scrawled on a moving wall. Four letters it had, but they wouldn't come together. This was the essence of man. A gibbering, slobbering thing and a four-lettered word on the undulating wall.

What was the word for scream?

"Four hours and fifteen minutes. Have you had enough, gentlemen?"

I'd had enough. The carpet, the red and yellow carpet, moved to meet the walls, the gray and black walls. The charcoal gray walls. The Madison Avenue walls.*

The sound was a knife in my throat. And I knew who was twisting the knife. I knew the son of a bitch who did it. Fetter me to a cross. To a double cross.

"We'll repeat the experiment tomorrow evening."

He stood up, a towering, terrifying figure. He lifted his hands in an evil benediction, his fingers waving like terrible tentacles. Two other figures moved toward me. They were giants with faces from an out-of-focus land.

"Lock him up and let it run its course. Tomorrow he can fit into the regular schedule after a routine examination. We'll run him through again tomorrow night."

They took me by the arms and helped me toward the door. My unarmed arms. Toward a doorway that changed sizes.

* Milo's mind seems to be free-associating from the charcoal gray of the walls to the "man in the gray flannel suit" who was the archetypal Madison Avenue conformist businessman of the 1950s and '60s.

The trick was to slip through fast while the doorway was big enough. Maybe I could slip through fast and let them be caught. I giggled.

They led me down the long corridor—the hallway that stretched and stretched and stretched all the way to Moscow. I could see the MVD at the end of it. Or maybe it stretched so far I could see the OGPU.*

They opened a door and pushed me inside. I fell to the floor, and the ceiling whirled like a merry-go-round. The door closed and the turning of the key was like thunder. Like thunder out of China across the bay.** Or maybe it wasn't across the bay anymore. A guy named Chou was changing all that. Chou was changing. Could you imagine knocking on a door and saying 'Chou sent me'?*** Or knocking on an Iron Curtain. What the world needed was more iron and less curtains.

Giggling to myself, I inched across the floor to the bed. I pulled myself up on it and huddled away from the prying eyes. There must be prying eyes somewhere. There had been.

But the eyes were gone. They'd locked the door. They were no more.

---

* Obyedinyonnoye Gosudarstvennoye Politicheskoye Upravleniye (Joint State Political Directorate), the Soviet secret police from 1923 to 1934, prior to the MVD.
** The line comes from the poem "Mandalay" (1892) by Rudyard Kipling (where it reads "An' the dawn comes up like thunder outer China 'crost the Bay!"). The poem was set to music in 1907 and became a hit as sheet music in America; it was later recorded by several artists. Mandalay is a city of Burma. The "Bay" in the line refers to the Bay of Bengal, but Kipling's geography was wrong, as that bay was not actually across from China. Milo's rambling thoughts allude to Burma's apprehensions about Communist Chinese intentions, though Premier Chou En-lai made a friendly visit to Burma in 1954.
*** The name of the first premier of the People's Republic of China (Chou En-lai or Zhou Enlai) is pronounced *Joe*. The phrase "Joe sent me" is associated with Prohibition, when supposedly the phrase was used to gain admittance into a speakeasy.

There was something I had to do. Something that would make everything go away and make me Milo March again. It was something important. I struggled with the shadows and tried to think. To think was an obscenity on a moving wall—I choked that off. There was something important.

I remembered what it was. I sat up on the bed, clawing at my crotch. The buttons on my shorts weren't buttons. They were locks. Big locks. But my fingers were the keys. I struggled with them and finally they fell away. I found the bag and pulled at the tape. It ripped away. The pain was sweet.

I looked around the room—the room with the waving walls. Every room equipped with hot and cold running walls. There was a little sink and a glass. A plastic glass so nobody could hurt himself. A plastic obscenity glass. I went across the room. A long way. The sink was free-shaped. Free-shaped in a slave state. I got some water—water that ran with a roar that hurt my ears. I clawed little pills out of the bag and crammed them into my mouth. The water washed them down my throat. My throat that wasn't mine. My throat closed hungrily on the pills. I went back across the room to the dancing bed.

There was something else I had to do. Something just as important. What was it? I asked myself—the myself that wasn't me. There was something to think about. I examined the thought.

Examination. That was it. The big one, the son of a bitch, had said I was to be examined. They'd find them. I had to save the pills. Examined. They'd find them. There was an old joke. Be sure the doctor doesn't have both hands on your shoulders.

Giggling, I rolled off the bed. I lifted the mattress, and clawed at it. After a while—how many hours and minutes since the drug was administered, Herr Doktor?—there was a hole. I stuffed the bag and the pills into the hole. The mattress flopped down. The pills were important. They would do something for somebody. I crawled back on the bed.

Then I waited. I was waiting for something. I closed my eyes and watched the pretty colors. After a while they faded. I opened my eyes. The ceiling was a dirty white. It wasn't moving.

I slept.

NINE

Sleep left me slowly. Finally I opened my eyes. I was in a strange room. It was painted a dirty white. There was a small sink and a simple toilet. A plastic glass was on the floor near the sink. I had never seen this room before.

Then my memory returned with a painful rush. This was the room into which they had pushed me after some four hours under the influence of LSD. I had pulled myself, giggling wildly, up on this bed. I had gotten out the chlorpromazine pills and found my way across to the sink. I had swallowed some of them and come back and hidden the rest of them in the mattress of the bed. I got out of bed and lifted the mattress. They were still there.

The night before, when I'd realized that I would have to take the drug and go through it without the antidote, I had some idea that I wouldn't be able to remember much when I came out of it. I thought it would be a little like a bad drunk, with occasional snatches of memory and the rest of it a merciful blank. But it wasn't like that at all. I could remember every illusion, every hallucination, in complete detail—all the distorted figures, the walls that closed in, the undulating floor. And somehow it was even more frightening, remembering it, than it had been in experiencing it. Frightening that such things could be made to happen to a person. It seemed like the final assault on the individual.

Remembering made me certain of one thing. I couldn't go through it again. I was just as aware as I had been the night before that there were others—among them Hermann Gruss— who had gone through it many times, but I couldn't. Maybe there were other things I could stand that they couldn't, but this schizophrenia bit wasn't for me.

Sometime before they came for me I was going to swallow a handful of the chlorpromazine and then try to act out the schizophrenic state. Maybe I could carry it off. If I couldn't, they might cart me off to a nice safe jail.

The door opened and two attendants came in. They were also Russian, I realized as soon as one of them spoke. It was proof that Moscow was taking Oderbruch's experiments seriously.

"He's awake," one of them said to the other. "He recovers quickly."

"Why the hell shouldn't I?" I growled. "I'd like to get some clothes and some breakfast."

"He speaks Russian," the first one said in surprise. "I didn't know any Americans knew our language."

"You'd be surprised what I can do," I said. "In the meantime, I'd like a little service around this place. How about it?"

"Later, little one," the Russian said. "Everything will come in good time. First, you come with us."

"How about some clothes?" I demanded. I had torn all but one of the buttons off my shorts the night before. They'd stay up, but I'd feel a little better with more on me.

"You don't need them yet," he said. "First, you have to see the doctor. He prefers that you don't wear too much."

They marched me out of the room and down the hall. I began to feel I'd been along that damn hall enough times to own part of it. They took me to the end of the corridor and into a doctor's office. The doctor soon showed up. I didn't know him. And I'd been right in leaving the pills hidden in my room. He gave me a thorough examination. When the doctor was through with me, they gave me some clothes. Pants and shirt of brown denim, rough cotton socks, and something that was a cross between shoes and slippers. No laces in them. There was no belt for the pants either. None of the clothes fit too well, but I was so glad to get them that I didn't make any complaint.

After that they led me down to the other end of the corridor, where we took the elevator down to the main floor. They herded me into the first door. It turned out to be a large dining room, filled with long tables and benches. There must have been about a hundred men there eating breakfast. All of them were dressed as I was.

One of the attendants nudged me. "Go over there," he said, "and get a tray and utensils. Then go along the railing and you'll get your breakfast. Sit down any place you want to."

I saw the long railing in front of a counter. Two men stood back of the counter, although now there weren't any customers. At one end there was a stack of trays. I went over and took one. Next to the trays were some big bowls and coffee mugs and spoons. I took a bowl and a mug and two spoons. Then I stepped down to where the two men waited. One of them filled the bowl with oatmeal and slid a little pitcher of milk onto my tray. The other one filled the mug with coffee.

I was surprised to see that it looked like pretty good coffee. I was about to move on when one of the men spoke in German.

"Here," he said. "Don't you want these?" He was holding up a package of cheap German cigarettes and matches. I nodded and he tossed them onto my tray.

I went over to the nearest table. There was an empty place at one end. I put the tray on the table and sat down. I realized I was hungry. I looked around the table. There were several bottles of sugar on it. I snared one and shook some on my oatmeal and in my coffee. Then I tried the milk.

There was another surprise for me. I'd expected the oatmeal to be the watery kind you get in prisons, but it wasn't. It was pretty good stuff. Not that I'm an oatmeal fancier. The way I look at it, once you've eaten oatmeal, you've had it. They should have kept it in Scotland. But I was hungry enough to eat it all. And the coffee was good.

While I sipped the coffee and smoked a cigarette, I looked around. Most of the men were doing the same thing I was. Practically none of them was talking, except those who were at the other end of the room.

At first, I thought all the men looked pretty much alike and were dressed exactly the same. Now I began to notice differences. About half of the men, those at the other end of the room, wore the same brown denim, but there was a broad red stripe slanting across both arms of their shirts. And they looked healthier and more alert than the rest of the men, the ones without the red bar. I looked again at my own shirt. No red stripes.

Maybe, I thought, the red-striped ones were some kind of graduates. With degrees of Bachelor of Schizophrenia.

There didn't seem to be much regimentation about the place. I noticed men from both sides of the room get up and saunter out through the various doors. I decided to try it myself. I finished my coffee and headed for the nearest door.

It didn't work quite the same way for me. The same two attendants were waiting there for me.

"Where to now?" I asked. "Back to the cage?"

"Just one more little routine to go through," one of them said. His attitude was still very impersonal, as though he herded guys like me around all day and didn't much care who it was.

We walked down a corridor again. We turned in to what seemed to be a large office, went through it and into a small, private office. The man behind the desk wore the uniform of a captain in the Russian Army. He looked up and nodded at me. His attitude was neither friendly nor unfriendly.

"You speak Russian?" he asked.

"Yes," I said.

"Good. What is your name?"

"Milo Nalyevo," I said, sticking to the name on my forged identity card. It wasn't really important, but it might help in the propaganda exchanges that would take place if I escaped. If.

He looked at me patiently. "It will accomplish nothing for you to act in this manner. We know who you are. This is just for the record. Now, what is your name?"

"For the record—Milo Nalyevo."

He shrugged and made a notation on the paper in front of him. "Your rank?"

"Lieutenant. In the MVD."

Another notation. "Name and address of nearest of kin?"

"Bulganin," I said. "The Kremlin, Moscow—providing he hasn't moved. I haven't seen the morning papers."

He put down his pencil. "This is really very foolish. We know that you are Milo March, a major in the Army Reserves, recently recalled to active duty and assigned to the Central Intelligence Agency. Your nearest of kin is Greta March, your wife, who formerly lived in East Berlin, and we have her current address in Denver, Colorado. We know why you were sent here and we know all about your last mission to East Germany."

"It's getting just impossible to keep a secret anymore," I said. "Everybody's turning into an amateur Peeping Tom."

He shrugged again. "That's all," he said.

The attendants herded me back to the corridor.

"You really should be more cooperative," one of them said.

"Look," I told him, "I was cooperative enough last night to do me for a long time. If I ever feel like being cooperative again, which I doubt, I'll send you an engraved invitation."

"All right," he said. "We can't stand around here talking about it all day. We'll be seeing you."

That caught me off base. "What do you mean, you'll be seeing me? Am I supposed to stand here in this damn corridor all day?"

"Of course not. Do anything you want to."

"Anything?"

"Anything you can," he said with a grin. "There's a recreation hall across from the dining room. Or you can go out in the grounds if you like. I think a look around, once you're out, will convince you that you're being given as much freedom as you can handle. You'll hear a bell announcing lunch and dinner. After lunch, you can do the same thing or go to your room and sulk if you want to. And that's your day until Dr. Oderbruch wants you sometime tonight."

The two of them marched away before I could ask any more questions. I looked around. There was nobody else in sight. It looked as if they meant it. I turned around and headed for the door.

There was a Russian soldier at the door, but he paid no attention to me. I began to feel that this was some new version of the Mexican prisoner escape, where I'd get a bullet in the back as soon as I stepped out. But it seemed almost worth the chance, so out I went. Nothing happened.

Once I was out on the ground, I saw what the attendant meant. The wall around the grounds was ten feet high and, I suspected, several feet thick. There were turrets on top of the wall every hundred yards, and in each turret there were two soldiers with machine guns. But that was only the beginning. On the inside of the wall, there were sentry boxes every hundred feet, and in each one there was a Red soldier with a machine gun. In addition to these, I saw several MVD men strolling around the grounds in an aimless fashion. It began to look like a Russian version of Fort Knox.

It looked as if most of the men who'd been to breakfast were now out on the grounds. Some were strolling around. Others were sitting on benches or on the grass in the cool shade of various big trees. Around on one side of the hospital there were several volleyball courts and handball courts. There were a number of men playing. I soon noticed that they were all those with the red bands on their arms.

Suddenly I thought of something. I'd been breaking my neck to think of some way of getting in here so I could reach Hermann Gruss. Now I was in. So was Gruss, presumably. I might as well spend some of this time looking for him. Even if I couldn't get him out, maybe I could slip him some of the chlorpromazine tablets. If he became convinced that his illness had also been caused by Oderbruch, maybe he'd start fighting back.

There was also a chance that he was too important a man to just let wander around. Especially, I thought, since somebody might always tip him off. The more I thought about it, the more I became convinced that Oderbruch would be smarter than that.

Meanwhile, I was wandering around. Although there must have been fifty of the men without stripes on their arms, I seldom saw even two of them talking together. They all seemed in rather low spirits and not especially interested in anything.

I finally walked up to one of them and spoke to him in German. I'd guessed the right language, at least. He answered me, but he seemed willing to let the conversation die right there.

"I'm new here," I explained. "Is the food always as good as it was at breakfast?"

"Oh, yes," he said. "They are very good to us here."

"Yeah?" I said. "What about all the Russkies with the popguns?"

He glanced at them without interest. "That's for our own protection. Some of us get a little violent once in a while."

"They're ready for a lot of violence," I said. "Tell me, what do they want you to confess?"

He looked at me as if I'd just flipped my lid in public. "I don't understand you," he said.

"Why are you in here?"

"For treatment, of course. I've been very ill."

"And you're not one of Oderbruch's experiments?"

He began to edge away from me as if he thought I might get violent any minute.

"The only experimenting Dr. Oderbruch does is with medicine to cure us. He is very hopeful, too."

"I'll bet. What is your sickness?"

He took a quick look at my shirt and pants. "All of us in here are suffering from schizophrenia."

"Not me. I—" I broke off, realizing that I was wasting my time. He was convinced that I was mentally ill or I wouldn't be there, and any attempt to tell him otherwise would only make him certain I was about to flip the rest of the way over. "What about the ones with the red stripes on their arms?"

"They must be the same," he said simply. "They're in here. They never talk to us, but they must be patients who have already come a long way toward recovery. I think, perhaps, they are brought here from other hospitals and then are sent home from here. They are never here long." He was still edging away from me.

"When did you first get sick?" I asked him.

"When I was in the Workers' Hospital. Dr. Oderbruch fortunately noticed the symptoms before I was even aware I was mentally ill. He had me brought here soon afterwards."

"And he doesn't give you a drug in plain water?"

"The only medicine I get is the same as everyone gets. The two pills. One to take when I get an attack and one to take in between attacks. I—I have to go now and tend my flowers. I'm growing some petunias on the other side of the hospital." He peered at me intently. "If you're all out of the pills for attacks, why don't you go see Dr. Eckholdt? He might give you another one." With that advice, he scuttled away.

I talked to two more of the men and got about the same answers and the same attitudes. And they all had two kinds of pills. If I was right about what was in those pills, Oderbruch was keeping all of these poor bastards bouncing in and out of insanity like yo-yos.

But I began to feel more hopeful about running across Gruss. It looked as if nobody could tip him off because they were all suffering the same delusion. Except me. But so far my attempts to say anything were only earning me the reputation of being on the point of blowing my stack.

I went looking for Gruss. I remembered him well enough from the photograph to spot him. And I finally did. He was around in the back of the hospital, sitting under a tree all by himself. I recognized him at once, even though his face was far more haggard than it had been when the photograph was taken. I went over and sat down a couple of feet away from him. He glanced at me as I took out a cigarette and lit it, but he looked away again.

"You're Hermann Gruss, aren't you?" I asked.

He looked at me again and I could see the pain and the terror in his eyes. But back of it, I could also see some of the intelligence that had made him what he had been. That was what I had to reach.

"Yes," he said. "You're new here, aren't you?" He didn't sound as if he really cared, but only as if he was trying to be polite.

"Yes," I said. I smoked for another minute in silence. "I'm an American," I added.

He looked at me with a little more interest, mixed with something that might have been contempt. "One of those who came over here some time ago?" he asked.

"No. I came into East Berlin only five days ago. In fact, I came all the way from America just to find you."

"Yes," he said flatly. His voice told me that he was humoring me.

"Yes," I said. "Look, I know that everyone in here is supposed to be a schizophrenic. Me, too. And last night for about five hours I guess I was one. But I was brought by the MVD, not a doctor. The reason was that they discovered who I was and why I was here."

He nodded in agreement without meeting my eyes. He didn't believe me any more than the others had, but he was too polite to edge away.

"You never met me," I said, "but did you ever hear of Milo March?"

He looked thoughtful for a minute, then nodded. "He was an American agent who broke into East Germany about two years ago and kidnapped an English scientist who had defected to the East."

"Right," I said. "I am Milo March. I don't have any identification on me, of course. But I'm a major in the United States Army Reserve. About nine days ago I was called to active duty and assigned to the Central Intelligence Agency. My assignment was to come into East Germany and return with you. I know that you were in America not long ago and that you were shown around the CIA. You must have also received reports on my trip into East Germany two years ago. I should be able to prove to you that I'm Milo March by knowing things that couldn't be picked up by just anybody."

He chewed that over for a couple of minutes. "Perhaps," he said finally.

"Which of the two?"

"I've always been interested in the American Central Intelligence Agency," he said.

"I received my assignment," I told him, "from Lieutenant General Sam Roberts, George Hillyer, and Philip Emerson. Hillyer is head of CIA and Emerson is his assistant. General Roberts is the head of Army G-2. The three of them make up the planning board of the Central Intelligence Agency."

"Almost anyone could know that," he said.

I struggled to think of something that would convince him. "I know that you were ill while you were in Washington and that there were several days you didn't show up. But you refused to see an American doctor. You had medicine that Oderbruch had given you, and you wouldn't try anything else." I was just babbling and I knew it. Then suddenly I had an idea. "When they were showing you around the CIA, did they tell you the setup on the first briefing of a new agent?"

"They might have."

Nobody had told me that what I'd gone through was the regular procedure, but I had an idea it was. In fact, I would have bet it had been cooked up by Sam Roberts. I took a chance that it was the regular routine and that they would have told Gruss about it.

"I was ordered to Washington," I said. "When I got there I was met with sealed orders, telling me to report to room three twenty-one in this office building. I went there and discovered there was no room three twenty-one. I wandered around on the floor for a while, making sure of it, then started to leave. At the elevators I ran into a pleasant young man—by accident, it seemed—who was very helpful. He tried to pump me. He was a G-2 character in plain clothes. I don't know what would have happened if I had been pumpable—probably I would have been reassigned somewhere else and would never have known what happened. But I didn't fall for the sucker-bait, so he finally told me that I was expected in room three sixteen. While I was in there, he came in and reported on me. I doubt very much if that is general knowledge."

"All right," he said listlessly. "I'll grant that you're from the CIA. But that doesn't prove that you're Milo March."

"Granted," I said, "but if you believe I'm from the CIA, that's the important thing. It doesn't matter whether you think I'm Milo March or some other agent."

"You're right, it doesn't matter," he said, "but not for the reasons you think. It doesn't matter because I came to East Berlin voluntarily and I'm staying voluntarily. There is nothing to rescue me from."

"Maybe. All I'm asking you to do is listen to me."

"I'm listening."

"Look," I said. "Dr. Oderbruch is a Communist agent. He was one even back in the days when you and he were in the German underground together. It was Oderbruch who tipped off the Nazis about the bomb plot against Hitler. He told me this himself. Lately, he has been experimenting with drugs for the Communists. One of the drugs is lysergic acid diethylamide. It produces every symptom of schizophrenia."

"What you are saying about Franz is nonsense," he said. "Franz is my best friend and has been for more than twenty years. He would not do what you are implying. I would stake my life on that."

"You already have," I said, "but he's still doing it. Oderbruch is giving you two kinds of medicine, isn't he? One that you take between attacks and one you take when an attack is coming on?"

"Yes."

"Well, the one you take in between is what brings on the attacks. The other is a drug that will stop it."

"I don't believe it."

"When did you have your first schizophrenic attack?" I asked.

"Perhaps ten months ago."

"Did you have any warning of it?"

"Yes. I had been feeling very nervous and tense for some time, with headaches often. I told Franz about it. He warned me that it sounded as if I were already a borderline schizophrenic. He said it might be too late to stop it, but he gave me some medicine. He was right. It didn't stop it. I had my first attack right after that."

"How soon after?"

"The next day, I think."

"Which medicine did he give you first? The one that you take between attacks?"

"Yes."

"And you never had an attack before you took the medicine?"

"No."

"How often were the attacks at first?"

"I'm not sure. Perhaps once every week or ten days."

"And did you take the medicine every day then?"

"No," he said.

"How often are the attacks now?"

"Daily."

"You started taking the medicine more often and the attacks increased accordingly," I said.

"You're twisting it around," he retorted. "I started having more attacks, so the frequency of the medicine was increased."

"Maybe," I said. "Did you ever have an attack when you hadn't taken the medicine?"

"I don't know. I can't be sure."

"Did you ever take the medicine and not have an attack?"

He thought a minute. "I—I don't think so."

"How do you get the medicine?"

"I always have a large supply of the first medicine. When it gets low I can get more. The second medicine, the one that stops the attacks, is scarce. Also, it would be dangerous to take too many, which I might do in the panic of an attack. One is issued each day. When I went to America, Franz gave me a supply of one for each day I would be gone, but cautioned me about them."

"The second medicine is chlorpromazine," I said. "It's not especially scarce at all."

"Whatever it is," he said stubbornly, "it does everything that Franz claims for it. It always stops an attack within an hour or so. Once I didn't have any, and I was in for seven or eight hours. I tell you I don't know what I would do if I had to go through that much every time."

"Did you ever do any reading on schizophrenia?" I asked.

"A couple of articles Franz showed me. I do not care to read it; I have been in it."

"Real schizophrenia," I said, "is not so self-limiting as to last only seven or eight hours; schizophrenic-like symptoms induced by LSD do last just that long. If you were really a schizophrenic, you might be in it for days and I doubt if you'd ever be completely out of it. Nor would the attacks come like such clockwork. When do you take the first medicine?"

"Just before dinner each day."

"And when do the attacks come?"

"Usually between eight and nine each night. Others have attacks at different times."

"Probably because they take their medicine at different times," I said. "Even an idiot might catch on if everyone in the hospital had their attacks at the same time. Is the first medicine in pill or capsule form?"

"Capsule."

That answered something that had bothered me about his last answer. I knew that the LSD had acted on me within less than thirty minutes; Gruss's time seemed close to three hours. But a capsule could explain that. All Oderbruch had to do was put the drug in a capsule that would dissolve after three hours in the stomach.

"Tell me something else, Herr Gruss," I said. "I know that you've given out some interviews to Communist newspapers and you've made a couple of radio broadcasts. You've given them some information, but not anywhere near as much as you could. I'd like to hear your explanation of this. If you're going to give them some information, why not all? If you don't want to give them any, then why give them part?"

For the first time he refused to look at me. "It is something of which I am ashamed," he said. "I doubt if you can understand. I came to East Berlin because Franz could treat me better here than in the West. The Communists have permitted it, but they are not pleased. They have objected to releasing the drugs which I need. The only way I have been able to get the drugs is by giving them information." He pulled up a few strands of grass and threw them away. When he spoke again his voice was defiant. "I'll do it again when I have to. I don't expect you to understand, but I'll do anything to keep from being permanently insane. You don't know what it's like."

"I had a small taste of it last night—at the hands of your friend," I said. "What does Oderbruch think about giving the Communists information?"

"He feels as I do about it, but he tells me there is no choice."

"Naturally. He gives you the medicine that turns you insane. Then he offers another medicine that relieves it, only the latter is scarce. Then he's so sorry, but you'd better turn over secrets so you can get the medicine."

"Franz is not a Communist," he said heatedly. "Oh, I'll admit that he may sometimes feel friendly toward them. He has been alarmed at the increase of neo-Nazism in the West. But so have I."

"So have I," I said, "but I haven't played footsie with the Communists. It doesn't do much good if you keep from being run over by a train only by dashing out in front of a truck. Look, Herr Gruss, you're supposed to be a good policeman. I've given you enough evidence. Look at it and tell me what you see."

He was silent for several minutes. "Go away," he said finally. "I don't believe you, but you have disturbed me. Please leave me alone."

"In a minute," I said. "There's no time for a long-drawn-out experiment or you could easily prove this. You could not take the capsule and you wouldn't have an attack. Then you could take it at a different time and watch the attack adjust to when you took the capsule. But there is another way to prove it to yourself quickly, if you'll do it."

"What is it?"

"The chlorpromazine, the drug that's so scarce. I have almost three hundred tablets of it. Hidden in my room. I'll get some of them to you this afternoon. Tonight when you have your attack, take more of them and you'll get over it quicker. Then, when it's had a chance to wear off, toward morning, take one of the capsules again. You'll find that an attack automatically follows. But you'll have enough chlorpromazine to stop it right away. If you prove to yourself that there's a relationship between the capsules and the attacks, that ought to make it clear."

He didn't answer me. He didn't want to believe any of this, but I knew he'd started thinking, and from what I knew about him, once the process was started, he wouldn't be able to stop it.

"Will you do it?" I asked.

"Bring me the tablets," he said heavily. "If they're the same as the ones I have, I'll do it."

I left him with that. I'd already done all I could at this stage. The rest was up to him and chlorpromazine.

I loafed the rest of the morning until the lunch bell sounded. Then I went in with the rest of the men. The lunch was good. There was even beer with it.

After lunch, I'd been told, we could go to our rooms. As soon as I'd finished eating, I headed for the elevator in the corridor. One of the attendants from that morning was standing beside the elevator.

"Where are you going?" he asked as I came up.

"To my room. You said that it was all right after lunch."

"Where is your room?"

"On the fourth floor. I don't know as it had a number, but I can find it. It was the twelfth door on the left from the elevator."

"That's not your room now," he said. "You're on the third floor. The room is three-E."

"What was wrong with my room on the fourth floor?" I demanded. "I liked it."

"No one lives permanently on the fourth floor. It's used only for newcomers and Dr. Oderbruch's work. You'll get to see it again tonight when the doctor wants you." He grinned at me.

There was no point in arguing. That would only make him suspicious. So I went on up to the room on the third floor. It was exactly like the other one—except that there were three hundred chlorpromazine tablets in the mattress on the fourth floor. I needed them to convince Gruss—and I was going to need them later for myself.

I sat and brooded for a while and then decided that wasn't going to get me anyplace. I checked on the corridor. There weren't any attendants around. I went out and scouted around. I finally found one thing I was looking for, a door that opened onto a stairway. It undoubtedly led up to the fourth floor. There was only one thing wrong with it. When I opened the door and looked in, the first thing I saw was an attendant. He was sitting in an easy chair and reading a magazine, but he was obviously there to keep anyone from going upstairs. I apologized for my mistake and retreated.

I went back to my room. I was sure that when night came I'd probably be locked in, so I examined my door. The lock on it was a fairly simple one, but the only keyhole was on the outside. It would be impossible to pick the lock from the inside even if I could get tools.

Finally, I went back downstairs. I didn't have any ideas, but I'd be more apt to get one moving around than sulking in my room. On the ground floor, I wandered around until I finally spotted one of the attendants I knew. He wasn't busy at the moment and I got him to talking. After a while I got in the question I was the most interested in.

"What time," I asked, "will Dr. Oderbruch be around tonight?"

"You're in luck," he said. "Dr. Oderbruch phoned just a few minutes ago to say he won't be here tonight. Something has come up." He must have seen the relief on my face for he laughed. "Don't worry, *Amerikanka*. You're still going to get your medicine. We'll give it to you just before we tuck you in for the night."

That was a big help! I traded a few more idle remarks with him and then beat it. I went out on the grounds and found Gruss. I told him there'd been a slight change in plans, that I couldn't get him the chlorpromazine right then, but I'd bring it to him that night. I found that he was on the third floor only a few rooms away from me. I don't think he believed me, but we left it at that.

Then I began rather aimlessly getting acquainted with the grounds and the hospital. From one of the other men, I learned that there was a shop in the hospital and that each of us was allowed stuff from it amounting to the equivalent of about a dollar a week. All the comforts of home.

I went in and investigated the shop. It carried a lot of simple necessities, little cheap things that could be used to decorate a room, and plenty of magazines and cheap books. Nothing that anybody could hurt himself with. There were even some toys. Maybe they were supposed to be play therapy. One toy made me almost think I was back home. It was a Slinky toy, the coil of steel wire that will walk downstairs.

After I looked around in there for a little while I began to feel better. I finally picked out a cheap pocket comb in a celluloid case and a Slinky toy. The man behind the counter marked them down against my name. I stuffed them in my pocket and went back out on the grounds.

I spent the rest of the afternoon stretched out under a tree, trying to look like just another happy inmate.

Dinner was just as good as the other two meals had been. Unless you dug in under the surface, it seemed to be a mental hospital where they treated the patients with every consideration. Everybody there was so concerned with himself that nobody even wanted to look beneath the surface. Except maybe the guys with the red stripes on their arms. I was curious about them. I had a hunch they were part of the other special work Oderbruch had mentioned.

After dinner I went up to my room. As soon as I was inside, I went to work. I took the celluloid comb case and tore it into strips. It took me a little longer with the Slinky toy, but I finally had two pieces broken out of it. They weren't quite as good as keys, but they were thin enough and strong enough to perform a few miracles.

I put everything away and waited.

It was about seven o'clock when the door opened and the attendant came in. It was one of the Russians. He was carrying a glass of water, already spiked, I was sure, with LSD. He handed it to me.

"Here," he said. "Pleasant dreams." The idea seemed to amuse him greatly.

"Why do I have to take it?" I asked. "If Oderbruch isn't coming, why can't I just skip it?"

"Doctor's orders," he said. "He likes to get you in the habit. Come on. Down with it.'

He was being friendly enough, but the implied threat was there. I turned the glass up and drank it. I handed him the empty glass.

"I'll see you in your dreams," he said. He was a very funny man. For a Russian.

As he closed the door, I was off the bed and leaping across the room. The door was barely shut when I had a strip of celluloid in between the door and the doorjamb. I held it there while the lock turned.

Then I waited. I didn't have much time. Maybe twenty-five minutes before the drug began to hit me, an hour before it got bad. Before that happened, I had to get upstairs and into the room I'd been in the night before.

I gave myself ten minutes, counting the seconds off and watching to see that I didn't hurry the count. When I reached the six hundredth second, I pulled gently on the door, holding the celluloid in place. The door came open. I listened first. I didn't hear any sound from the corridor. Finally, I looked out. It was deserted. I stepped out and pulled the door almost shut. Unless someone looked closely, he wouldn't notice that it was partly open.

I went quickly down the corridor. There was a dull, moaning sound from one of the doors as I passed. Somebody's attack had started.

When I reached the stairway door, I opened it a couple of

inches, not far enough to see the guard or for him to see me.

"We need help," I said in Russian. "Three of the patients are loose." I stepped back and waited.

He came through the doorway, looking to see who had called him. As he turned his head, I struck with the edge of my palm at the base of his brain. He sighed heavily and slid to the floor. I picked him up and dragged him back into the stair-well. I left him there beside his chair and ran up the stairs.

It had been fifteen minutes since I took the drug.

I eased open the door on the fourth floor and looked out. There was no one in sight. I ran down the corridor to the twelfth door from the elevators. I tried the knob. It was locked. I got out my two pieces of steel wire and went to work.

It was a race against time in two ways. The drug limited my time and so did the possibility of someone showing up. The sweat rolled down my face as I prodded and twisted at the lock.

Finally, I hit it and the lock slid back. I opened the door, stepped inside quickly, and closed it.

There was a man sitting on the bed, staring at me wildly. One glance was all I needed to tell that he was already under the influence of the drug.

"Don't come near me," he said. "You're some kind of a freak. Don't touch me. Don't—" He started to scream.

I stepped in and hit him on the point of the jaw. He fell back on the bed and was still.

Twenty-three minutes since I'd taken the drug. I could feel the coldness in my feet and legs.

I pushed him off the bed and pulled up the mattress.

I dug the bag of tablets out through the hole I'd made. I opened the bag and grabbed five or six. I rushed across the room and got some water to wash them down. Then I went back to the bed and sat on it. I held on to the sides of the bed and waited.

After maybe twenty minutes I knew I was going to be all right. My feet were still cold and my legs were shaking and there was a little distortion to my vision, but I knew it wasn't going to get any worse. The chlorpromazine would hold it there and then drive it back. In the meantime, I had to be moving. The guard in the stairwell wouldn't stay unconscious forever.

I looked out the door. The corridor was still deserted.

I slipped out and closed the door behind me. I felt sorry about clipping the poor guy in the room, but maybe I'd done him a favor. With what he was going through, he was better off unconscious.

I was halfway down the hall when I heard a steady murmur of voices from behind one of the doors. It didn't sound like somebody in the middle of a schizophrenic dream. Besides, it sounded as if the speaker was using Russian instead of German. With the exception of me, it looked as if they were using only Germans in this experiment. I went over and eased open the door a couple of inches. I couldn't see in, but I could hear the speaker. He was speaking Russian, and it sounded like the captain I'd seen that morning.

"In a moment," he was saying, "I will take you in to see the special gymnasium. Some of the newest men will be working out there, then tomorrow you will be able to look over the entire setup. I am very sorry that Dr. Oderbruch couldn't be here tonight, but something very urgent came up in regard to a new drug we're getting from the West."

"Another deserter?" a heavy voice asked in Russian.

"Deserter or agent, I'm not sure."

"We've been very impressed, Captain Balabanoff," said the second voice, "with the reports we've received in Moscow on your work here. The other work that Dr. Oderbruch is doing is interesting, but we are more concerned with the special agents. I have read the reports, of course, but Colonel General Zinoviev here has not had the opportunity to do so. Would you briefly summarize the project for him?"

This sounded like the special project. I had to hear it if possible. I looked around. The corridor was still empty.

"Gladly," the Captain said. "The project, Colonel General, was started by this Dr. Oderbruch who has long been an agent of ours. He has been experimenting with a number of drugs, among them one known as chlorpromazine. It has many uses, but one of them is that, used in strong enough doses, it destroys all anxiety and fear. There are, however, a few individuals on whom it does not have this result. We have been receiving here the special squads of men who are selected for espionage and sabotage work. We put them through a testing period during which they are given the drug. Within two or three weeks we've weeded out those who have no reaction to the drug and found the correct dosage for the others."

"This is a mental hospital?" a third voice asked.

"In a way," the captain said. "We run the special trainees through here just the same as if they were regular inmates.

They even wear the same clothes except for red stripes on their sleeves. Once we're through with them here, we send them on to Carinhall, where they get their regular training. And we send along information on the correct dosage of chlorpromazine for each man. As you will see, Colonel General, a man with the right amount of chlorpromazine in him will charge right into a firing gun with no fear in—"

I closed the door. I would like to have listened longer, but it was dangerous, and I'd heard enough. I remembered Farley in the Berlin office of the CIA talking about the problem of raids by men who were absolutely fearless. Here was the explanation of it. The agents were being trained at Carinhall—Goering's old estate—but the secret was Dr. Oderbruch and chlorpromazine. I was beginning to think it was more important to take Oderbruch back to West Berlin than Gruss.

I crossed the corridor and hurried down the stairs. I was just in time, too. The guard was already stirring and moaning. I chopped my hand across his neck again and he was quiet.

The third-floor corridor was clear, too. I went down it until I came to Gruss's room. As I suspected, it was locked. I got busy with my two pieces of steel wire and in a couple of minutes the door was open. I stepped inside and closed it.

Gruss was on the bed and I could see that he was already in the first stages of schizophrenia. It was more evident in the panic I could see in his eyes than in anything else. He tried to control it at the sight of me, but he wasn't too successful.

"How did you get in?" he asked.

I held up the two strands of wire. "Mother's Little Helper," I said. I went straight across the room and filled his glass with water. I came back with it and shook out five of the orange tablets for him. "Sorry I'm late," I said. "There were a few obstacles. Here, take these."

He took the pills and gulped them down with water.

"How far along are you?" I asked.

"Vision," he said. "Your face looks like one of the gargoyles on the Notre Dame in Paris." I could see he was wanting to giggle but was controlling it.

"It's looked like that to me for years," I said. I sat down on the bed beside him and lit a cigarette. "Those extra pills will keep it from going any farther and will stop it faster. I've got a little dose of it myself."

"You?"

"Yeah. I get mine in a glass of water. They give me a choice. I can drink it down or take it from a needle while they hold me. They're softening you up to spill everything you know. They're softening me up for a grand-slam confession at a public trial."

He covered his face with his hands and peered out through the slits between his fingers. "Why?"

"Because I'm an American Army officer and they caught me in East Berlin in the uniform of an MVD officer. What's the difference? They owe me one from two years ago.... Look, I'm going to give you a fistful of these. You'll make the experiment in the morning as you agreed?"

He nodded.

"Okay." I dumped a handful of the orange tablets on the bed. "Hide them somewhere. I'll see you tomorrow." I checked on the corridor before I stepped outside. Then I stopped long enough to lock his door again. I went back to my own room. The door was the way I'd left it, so they hadn't discovered it yet. I went in and used the piece of celluloid to shut the door. Then I wriggled the celluloid loose and drew it out, letting the lock click into place.

After that, I used a match to burn up all the pieces of celluloid. I crumpled up the two pieces of wire and put them in the toilet. I had to leave the Slinky, but they might not pay any attention to it. Besides, I might need more wire.

Then I went to sleep.

TEN

It was my sixth day in East Berlin. It was beginning to feel like my sixth year. I woke up feeling a little better than I had the day before, but still feeling worse than even the hangovers had left me. It was probably from the battle of drugs that had taken place in my body the night before. As soon as my door was unlocked, I went down to breakfast. I didn't see Gruss anywhere, but I didn't want to make it obvious by looking too closely. I sat at the first table where there was space and ate my cereal. My companions weren't much peppier than they'd been the day before, but there was a little more talk. It seems that earlier there had been some slight hubbub over the guard who'd been clobbered the night before. Latrine gossip had it that the incident was blamed on some new guy on the fourth floor whose door had been accidentally left unlocked. He was in the middle of an attack, which was supposed to have been the cause. They hadn't done anything to him, but the attendant who left the door unlocked was in trouble.

The door was an oversight on my part, but maybe it was just as well. The other way, there might have been more of a rhubarb. The guard must have been pretty fuzzy, too, for nobody had stopped to figure out how the guy from the fourth floor got down to the third floor to call the guard. I was willing to let it go at that.

Later, out on the grounds, I went on a search for Gruss. I didn't find him. I didn't see him at lunchtime either, but about an hour later he showed up on the grounds. He spotted me sitting under a tree and came over. His face was drawn and haggard, as though he'd just been through a rough time, but he looked more alert than he had the day before.

"I think perhaps I owe you an apology, Major March," he said as he came up. "I don't know how I can redeem myself."

"I gather," I said, "that you tried the little experiment this morning and that it worked?"

He nodded. "But that isn't all. I am allowed even extra privileges here, so about an hour ago I telephoned Franz at his office. I told him what had happened and the things you had told me. He didn't deny it. He just laughed at me."

"I'm not too surprised," I said gently.

"For more than twenty years he is supposed to have been my friend," Gruss exclaimed. "Then he does this thing to me and, when I tell him I know, he laughs at me."

"I expect," I said, "that once he got you here, he kept up the pretense only because it amused him. There was no need. He can give you the drug by injection as well as any other way. And I expect continual exposure to schizophrenia can be just as frightening when you know how it's done as when you don't. I went through five hours of it night before last and I can tell you that I couldn't guarantee what I might eventually do if I had to keep going through it."

I don't think he'd heard anything I said. "But what I've done," he said. "I've betrayed my country, betrayed the West. How can I ever undo this terrible thing?"

"There will be plenty who will feel the same way about it," I told him, "but I think we can make some of them understand—even if I have to give a guy like General Roberts a dose of LSD myself. Providing, of course, that we ever get out of here."

"We must get out," he said, looking around as if he were seeing the place for the first time.

"I've been saying the same thing to myself since I arrived," I said. "Unfortunately, I forgot to bring a regiment of Marines with me. I hate to be disloyal to the Army, but I think it's Marines that are required in a situation like this. At least, it always is in the movies I see."

He glanced at me. "You joke?"

"I joke," I admitted. "It's a habit I fall into when I can't think of anything practical. You have any ideas on how to get out?"

He glanced around him again. "No," he said. "It looks difficult."

"Formidable, as a French friend of mine would say," I said. "Besides, there's another small item I would like to include in our plans to leave."

"What?"

"Dr. Franz Oderbruch. Bringing him back with you was part of my original orders, but I've sort of taken a personal interest in that part of them since night before last."

His face lit up. "I, too, would like that."

"I thought you might. Did Oderbruch mention when he was coming here?"

"Yes. He said he would be here in an hour or so. He mentioned something about bringing another important visitor from the West."

"Another prisoner?"

"He didn't say. I'm afraid I was too disturbed to think about asking."

"Well, we might as well wait and see. I don't think we're going anywhere in the meantime."

We sat under a tree where we could watch the front gates and we talked about ways of escaping from New Lenin Hospital. We both had plenty of ideas. The only trouble was that none of them would work. We needed something a little more threatening than just our brains. I did have one little idea which I didn't mention, simply because I couldn't see any way of getting it started. Even a cap pistol would have been a big help.

"Maybe," I suggested, "we ought to just call the CIA in West Berlin and say come and get us."

I was joking again, but he shook his head seriously. "I tried that," he said. He saw the look of surprise on my face. He smiled. "That is, I tried to call West Berlin. There is a public phone in the employees' lounge on the first floor. You can reach West Berlin from many public phones with only the danger of chance listening in by operators. I told you that I have had many special privileges here. One of them was admission to that lounge. But Franz must have alerted the hospital after our phone conversation. An attendant caught me just as I was entering the phone booth."

I laughed. "That would have been funny if you had succeeded. I knock myself out trying to think of something and you drop a few pfennigs into a phone and call the cops. Not that it would have done much good. All our people could have done was try to work through channels. They could have whisked us off to Siberia while the negotiations were going on.... Somebody's coming in now."

The big front gates were slowly opening. A snappy-looking Cadillac convertible rolled through and was waved on by the soldiers. It pulled up in front of the hospital.

Dr. Oderbruch was at the wheel, all right. That didn't surprise me. When I saw the car, I guessed it would be his.

But there was a surprise in the car for me. Sitting next to the doctor was Henri Flambeau.

My first thought was that he was a prisoner. But I soon saw that was wrong. The two of them climbed out of the car and strolled into the hospital together like old friends.

My second thought was a more unpleasant one. There was undoubtedly someone in the CIA office in West Berlin who was a spy. It was difficult not to connect this up with what I'd just seen. But I'd liked Henri and I forced the thought out of my head until there could be more evidence.

"There is something wrong?" Gruss asked.

"I don't know," I said. "I know the man with Oderbruch— only I don't know whether he's a friend or a foe."

"He looked as if he was a friend of Franz," Gruss said. "What do we do now?"

"Sit tight, I think," I said. "For a while. We've got to get to Oderbruch. But I know there are two important Russians in there waiting to see him, too. We need to see him in more privacy."

"I would like to get my hands on him."

"You will—only put them on gently. We want to take him

back to West Berlin. I think that when Oderbruch is through with the important visitors, he may send for one of us, perhaps both. If he doesn't, then we'll go looking for him."

"You have a plan?"

"No," I said grimly. "The only thing I can think of is getting hold of Oderbruch and bluffing our way out. But that's a pretty damn big bluff. Oderbruch's got all the cards. We haven't been dealt much. We'll have to play them pretty close to our chests, and even then we may not have enough for a good game of solitaire."

It was maybe thirty minutes later when Oderbruch again appeared. Henri was with him and so were the two Russians I'd heard talking the night before. They were all decked out in dress uniforms and medals. One of them was a major, the other a colonel general.

The four of them strolled around the grounds while Oderbruch obviously explained everything. They finally ended up about twenty feet from us. They stopped and stared at us solemnly.

"The heavyset one," Oderbruch explained, "is Hermann Gruss. You have heard all about him."

Beside me, Gruss tensed. I nudged him. "Sit still, you fool," I said in an undertone. "That would ruin everything." He subsided.

"The other one," Oderbruch said in an amused tone, "is the American spy they sent to rescue Gruss. As you can see, he has found him." They all laughed at this. "You should recognize him, Herr Flambeau."

"Oh, I do," Henri said. "That is March, all right." He left

the others and walked over to where I sat. He leaned over and spat on my foot. "American pig," he said. He turned and walked back to join the others.

"A little later," Oderbruch said, "I hope you can spare the chance to see both of them as part of the experiment." The four men walked on, with Oderbruch gesturing at another group of men.

"You should have gotten up and killed him for that, no matter what happened," Gruss said. "That was the man who was supposed to be your friend? Like my friend Franz."

"I would have liked to get up and kiss him," I said. "Look." I reached down and picked up a tiny ball of paper, no larger than a pea, that had rolled between my legs. Henri had shot it with his thumb as he leaned over to spit. I unrolled it carefully and squinted at the tiny handwriting:

My dear Milo: With great bravery and fortitude I have gotten into the place. Now how do we get out? After we have finished this delightful tour of your country home, I understand that we are to be in conference in some room on the fourth floor of this accursed building. I hereby invite you. No black tie. I have certain accessories, but no ideas. Your fellow exile, Henri.

When I'd finished reading it, I passed the note to Gruss. He read it and looked at me. "Do you know where they're having the conference?"

"I think so. It's probably the place where Oderbruch gave me a taste of schizophrenia while he lectured to three visiting firemen."

"What does he mean by 'accessories'?"

"I don't know," I said. "I can only hope he means weapons—preferably a few machine guns."

We waited, watching the four men. Finally, they went back into the hospital. I waited fifteen minutes, then got to my feet.

"Let's go," I said.

"Where to?" he asked, obediently standing up.

"To our rooms—ostensibly."

We went in and took the elevator to the third floor. There was an attendant walking along the corridor. I nudged Gruss and we each went into our own room. I listened at the door until the footsteps died out. Then I stepped back into the corridor. Gruss was out of his room almost as quickly. I motioned him to follow me and headed for the door to the stairwell.

"There is a guard in there," he whispered.

"I know," I said. "I became acquainted with the one that was on duty last night. I'm going to try a small variation on this one. You wait here."

I opened the door and looked in. The guard was standing about four feet away. He looked at me suspiciously.

"Excusez-moi de vous interrompre, mais on vous appelle au téléphone," I said rapidly. I could have said anything. He was Russian and I was gambling that he wouldn't know any language except his own.

"Chto vy skazali?" he asked.

Wearing my most ingratiating smile, I stepped through the door.

"Beregityes!" he said sharply.

I took one more step, which was enough. *"Merci, c'était juste ce qu'il me fallait,"* I said as I hit him. I caught him as he fell and eased him to the floor. Then, just to make sure of our time, I leaned down and hit him again, this time with the edge of my palm on his neck.

I opened the door and nodded to Gruss. We stepped around the guard and went up the stairs. The fourth-floor corridor was clear. We went rapidly down the hall until we came to the door which I remembered from the night before. There was a murmur of voices from the other side.

"I don't know what will happen when we go in," I whispered to Gruss. "It'll probably depend on Henri's accessories. But we'd better be ready for anything. When we go through, I'll go to the left and you go to the right so we won't represent a single target. After that we'll have to play it by ear."

He nodded. He had become a changed man in the last few minutes. Knowing that he was not really insane had snapped him out of the apathy in which I had found him.

I opened the door and went in fast, darting to the left. Without looking around, I could see from the corner of my eye that Gruss had done as I told him. Oderbruch, Henri, and the two Russian officers were seated around the table, which was spread with papers. The sound of the door brought their eyes up. Henri immediately pushed back his chair and moved like a cat away from the table.

"What's the meaning of this?" Oderbruch demanded sharply. "Who let you two up here?"

"Henri," I said, "what about those accessories—or do we have to do this job by hand?"

He grinned and threw something. It came hurtling across the room and into my hands. It was a small, flat automatic. It felt like money from home.

"Do we give him one?" Henri asked, nodding toward Gruss.

"Yes," I said.

Another gun arched across the room and Gruss caught it. A third gun appeared in Henri's hand.

"Henri, mon petit chou," I said, "you are a veritable arsenal."

"I am happy that you added the last two syllables," he said. "I apologize for the size of the guns, but they will still kill a man, no?"

"They will kill a man, yes," I said happily.

"What is the meaning of this?" Oderbruch shouted. His face looked as if he were about to have an apoplectic stroke.

"This is known as the turned-tables gambit," I said. "In other words, you are hoist by your own petard and it couldn't happen to a nicer son of a bitch."

The major's right hand had been stealthily working its way toward the inside of his uniform jacket. I decided I'd better take notice of it before I had to create an international situation. "I wouldn't do that, Major," I said in Russian. "Not only is it dangerous to you, but I might miss you and kill the Colonel General by mistake."

He stopped, and I could tell that the Colonel General approved of his decision.

"What is this?" the Colonel General demanded. He knew damn well what it was, but he was trying to maintain some dignity. "We do not understand."

"It's the American spy," Oderbruch said.

"Herr Doktor Oderbruch is off his trolley," I said. "I am Lieutenant Nalyevo of the Russian MVD. Herr Gruss is a famous Communist convert. My friend Henri is a more recent convert. We are now staging a new revolution. Lenin promised that the State would wither away, and we are about to accomplish it."

"We have nothing to lose but our chains," Henri said happily.

"You can't get away with this," Oderbruch shouted. "You are mad. You have seen the place. You can't hope to get out."

"I think we will," I said. The vague idea I'd had earlier was now blooming. "I really hate to do it, but I must ask the Major and the Colonel General to remove their uniforms."

"Que c'est beau," Henri said.

The Major started to protest.

"Poskoreye, pozhalusta," I said, gesturing with the gun. The protest stopped.

"This will mean war," Oderbruch said. "A Frenchman and an American crossing national borders and kidnapping people."

"Nothing of the kind," I said. "There are two Germans and a Frenchman who deserted to the East, then changed their minds and went back. There is no American here at all—only a young lieutenant of the MVD who gets lost in the shuffle." I turned to Henri. "I love you like a brother. How did you turn up right here so opportunely?"

"It was nothing," he said with exaggerated modesty. With his left hand he whipped something from his pocket. "This morning's paper from West Berlin."

He was holding it up so I could see the headline: "French-man Defects to the East. Flambeau Takes New Insanity Drug to the Communists."

I looked my question.

"I got the message concerning the young man from Provence yesterday afternoon," Henri said. "Right away I put on my old clothes and slipped over here. I went to see the one who had sent the message. He told me where you probably were and gave me all the information you had told him about Oder-bruch's drugs. I went back to West Berlin and applied my mind to the problem."

"I thought you looked a little strained," I said.

"Ah! La belle affaire," he said. "So last night, I go to the CIA office and I break into a little safe in Farley's office and I take some samples of a new drug which is supposed to make insanity. I think it is same drug that Oderbruch has, but I know they will not release the name. I hide it well in my own office and take another little bottle, which I fill with water. It is this which I have been coyly promising to turn over to Herr Doktor."

"So that's how you got so chummy with Oderbruch and got brought here," I said.

"Oh, it is more than that. By good luck, Martin Lane, our security officer—you will recall him—comes into the office while I am there. So I punch him in the nose and make off. I went directly from our office to the MVD offices here on Unter den Linden. I arrived there at eight o'clock. And already they knew that I was coming and what I had stolen from Farley's office. Somebody had called them. And in this paper, it says that the badly assaulted Lane immediately called the police—but it was five minutes past eight when he called them."

I whistled. "So Lane has been the leak all along. Very pretty. Did Farley know what you were doing?"

"Nobody knows," he said. "I kept it all to myself so that there could be no leak about my real reason. As of this moment they still think that I am the traitor."

"Great," I said. "So now we also have to clear you when we get back."

By this time the two Russian officers had stripped off their uniforms. They looked much less impressive in their underwear. Gruss and I quickly took off our denim pants and shirts. Gruss put on the Colonel General's uniform and I put on the Major's. They weren't perfect fits, but they'd do.

We made the two Russians take off their underwear. We used those and strips torn from the pants and shirts Gruss and I had removed to gag them and tie them to the table.

Oderbruch stood by, looking exceedingly unhappy throughout all this. I knew what he was thinking. Even if they were rescued right then, the two Russians wouldn't be apt to forget that Oderbruch had been the cause of their being treated that way. Still, he probably preferred that to what awaited him in West Berlin, and he clung to the hope that he'd voiced before.

"You can't get away with this," he said again. "You won't be able to get out of the grounds."

"We will," I said. "You are going to drive the two Russians and the newcomer from the West out through the gates."

"And if you so much as blink," Henri promised, "you will get a bullet."

"It will be a pleasure," Gruss added. He hadn't taken his eyes off the doctor since he'd come in, and it was making Oderbruch nervous.

"It's going to be a little more complicated than that," I said. I walked around the room and came up behind Oderbruch. I searched him until I found the little metal case I'd seen two nights before. I opened it and took out the eyedropper. It was almost full of the colorless liquid.

I went over and got the pitcher of water and a glass. I poured water into the glass. Then I dropped a generous portion of the drug into the water.

"What's that for?" Oderbruch asked.

"For you," I said.

I thought he was going to faint. All of the color drained from his face and he put his hand on the table to steady himself.

"You put in at least a triple dose," he said weakly.

"I know," I said. "You're going to drink this now, Oderbruch. Then the four of us are going to walk down out of here and get into your car. We'll still shoot you if you try to give a warning, but not to kill. Only where it will hurt you. With this big a dose of LSD in you, even if you get to the chlorpromazine you'll still have to go through the madness you've been giving so many others. If you behave, as soon as we're out of the gate I'll give you all the chlorpromazine you want."

"You don't have any," he said.

"More than two hundred tablets," I told him. "All right. Drink this."

"You don't know what you're doing," he whimpered.

"Schizophrenia is one of the worst mental diseases to go through. It—it splinters a man—splits him into pieces."

"I know," I said grimly. "You put me through it once. And think how many times you put Gruss through it. It's high time you had a little firsthand information. Drink."

He took the glass, but his hand was shaking so badly I wasn't sure he wouldn't drop it. He managed, however, to get it to his lips and he drained the glass in convulsive swallows. He set the glass down on the table. A thin thread of spittle ran down his chin.

"Get me out of here," he said thickly, "so I can get the antidote."

"We're not leaving," I said, "until you pull yourself together. The way you're acting now would be a dead giveaway."

Somehow he managed it; it wasn't bravery, but fear. Still, within a couple of minutes, he was standing erect, his face a mask of Prussian stiffness.

"I am ready," he announced. His voice was that of a dead man.

The four of us marched from the room in close formation. Henri walked beside Oderbruch, while Gruss and I followed closely behind. Our automatics were small enough to be covered by a hand, so Gruss and I held them flat against our bellies. It probably made us look as if we were on parade, but then most Russian officers look like that anyway.

When we hit the first-floor corridor, Henri slipped his arm through Oderbruch's and began chatting gayly. I knew his gun was pressing against Oderbruch's ribs. On the way to the front we passed several attendants and a couple of Russian soldiers. They saluted us and that was all. I breathed a little easier when they were passed without any outcry, although actually I hadn't expected any. Soldiers are pretty much alike all over. When they meet big brass, they look at the rank and don't pay any attention to faces.

Oderbruch's car was still standing in front where he'd left it. The doctor opened the door and slid in under the wheel. He sat there stiffly.

"I'll get in front with him," I said. I slipped in next to him. Henri and Gruss got in the back.

"All right," I told Oderbruch. "Let's go. And don't make any mistake. As soon as we get to Treskow Allee, I'll give you the chlorpromazine."

A stubborn look came over his face. "How do I know you have any?" he said. "Maybe you're only telling me this."

I dug out the little cotton bag from my pocket and showed the orange pills to him. He started the motor.

We drove slowly down to the gate. The Russian soldiers snapped into salutes and then hurried to open the gates. We drove through. Oderbruch swung the car to the right, then quickly made a second right turn. It was about two blocks to Treskow and we made it quickly. Just before we reached it, Oderbruch jammed on the brakes and turned to me.

"Give them to me," he said hoarsely.

I handed over the bag. Without bothering to count, he poured out a handful and crammed them into his mouth. There was no water, of course, but he swallowed them, gagging in the process. When they were down, he leaned back against the seat and wiped the sweat from his face.

"Climb over the seat into the back," I said.

He obeyed without a question. Henri and Gruss slid apart, making room for him between them. I moved over under the wheel of the Cadillac. I searched the dashboard until I found the switch controlling the top. I pressed the button, sending the top arching backward.

"The less wind resistance we have, the better," I said, "and that top won't stop any bullets, although you'll have to watch Oderbruch closely to see that he doesn't jump out."

"He won't jump," Gruss said grimly.

"Why worry?" Henri said jubilantly. "All we do is now drive calmly into the West."

"Want to bet?" I asked.

The words were hardly out of my mouth when a siren split the air behind us. It was a big siren. It couldn't have been coming from any place except the hospital.

"You see what I mean?" I shouted. "There was a guard in the stairwell. He couldn't have stayed unconscious forever. Or maybe somebody walked in on the Russian brass."

I put the car in gear and swung to the left on Treskow.

"There's a car just coming out of the hospital," Henri shouted.

"We'll soon lose him," I said, "but from here on, you'd better hang on. They'll be telephoning ahead."

Gruss leaned forward. "Do you know how to reach West Berlin?' he asked.

"If they haven't changed the streets, I do. I'm going to take the shortest route even though that's what they'll expect us to do. I'm in a mood to follow Horace Greeley's advice."

"Greeley?" Henri asked.

"He was a journalist who once told all American young men to go to the West. I'll explain when I'm through driving."

I swung left on Hönower and tramped the accelerator to the floorboards. The big Cadillac surged forward. I could see an army car in the rearview mirror, but it soon faded out of sight.

Hönower swung around, following the curve of the surface railway, heading north. Even though it was swinging away from the West, it was the shortest way, for there was no direct route across the Spree River. This would bring us to the nearest bridge. Behind us, the siren faded away to a thin wail.

At Schlicht Allee I swung left, then right again on Haupt Strasse. As soon as we were past Rummelsburger See, I turned left again. Straight ahead of us was the bridge across the Spree. Even as we came into sight of it, two Russian soldiers ran out and started trying to close the gates. The roar of the Cadillac warned them that they were too late. They fell to either side, grabbing for their rifles.

The Cadillac hit the bridge and was gone before they could get into action. I didn't even bother to look in the mirror; I knew the trouble would be ahead. I could already hear a siren cutting down from the north on the other side of the Spree.

We came off the bridge doing ninety miles an hour. This is where Köpenicker divides to go around Treptower Park and then comes together again at the Teltow Canal. I swung slightly to the left to hit Eisen Strasse. Two black security cars were screaming down from my right, their sirens clearing the way. They were coming fast, but they were going to be too late. Then I saw it. Straight ahead on Eisen Strasse, two more security cars were pulled straight across the road, blocking it.

"Hang on," I yelled.

I pulled the steering wheel sharply to the right. The big Cadillac careened, threatened to tip over, and then straightened out. We hit the sidewalk with protesting springs, went over, and hit the grass of the park. I swung right again, letting the car skid on the grass, just missed a statue of some Red general, and bounced across a walk, spraying gravel in every direction.

I could hear the guns behind us, but the bullets weren't coming near—or if they were, I wasn't noticing them. Which was just as well.

The Cadillac bounced over another sidewalk and into Köpenicker. I swung it sharply to the right, the tires squealing loudly. A hundred yards on, we hit Eisen Strasse again, just beyond the roadblock they'd set up. As I swerved left on Eisen Strasse, the blocking cars were already swinging around in pursuit.

From here it was a straight run to the border, and I pushed the accelerator down as far as it would go. It was now a regular parade. There were six security cars strung out behind us—and not too far behind, either. Half of the windshield fell out of the Cadillac just in time to remind me of that.

"Get down," I yelled over my shoulder. "It won't be long now."

The Cadillac was doing a hundred miles an hour, and straight ahead was the border. The Russians had closed the gate, and I could see several soldiers lying alongside with their rifles. They had also tried to park a car in front of the gates, but it was only partway out. They hadn't had time to do a really good job.

I hunched over the wheel as far as I could and hung on. I wasn't too much afraid of the bullets. It's hard to hit a car going a hundred miles an hour. The real problem was that I had just barely enough space to squeeze that Cadillac through between the parked car and the sentry building. And there was the gate, probably with a chain across it.

I aimed the Cadillac for the building and then at the last second swung it to the right. I heard a fender scrape the building—then we hit the gate. The car seemed to buck for a minute, then surged on through. Pieces of wood showered through the air, one just brushing my ear.

We were in West Berlin.

A couple of blocks away there were two West Berlin police cars converging on us. I let the Cadillac roll. It went four or five blocks past the police cars before I brought it to a stop. When the cops arrived, I was trying to light a cigarette. There was something wrong with the match. It wouldn't hold still.

ELEVEN

The West Berlin police listened to my story with disbelief until one of them caught a good look at Gruss. He saluted automatically and then obviously wished there were some way to take it back. After that, they escorted us to the CIA without further argument.

It turned out to be quite a party before it got under way. The Central Intelligence Agency, the Army, the Navy, the Air Force, British and French Intelligence, and a dozen departments of the West German government. The first thing I did was see to it that Martin Lane was put under wraps.

After that I quickly told the whole story and turned over the lysergic acid diethylamide that was in Oderbruch's eyedropper and the chlorpromazine. Henri went in and dug up the stolen drug that he'd stashed in his office. Farley was tugging at my elbow, but I stayed around long enough to be sure that Henri was going to be cleared.

Farley rushed me into his private office. The wires were already burning up between Washington and his office. It seemed everybody was worrying about what was going to happen next. In a way we'd been caught red-handed and then I'd topped it off by assaulting two high Russian officers.

They snagged an unfortunate young Army lieutenant who was about my size and dragged him into the office. They made him strip off his uniform. I took off the Russian uniform and put on his. They borrowed some oak leaves from a major who was present and pinned them on my shoulders. Then they hustled me out the back way and into an Army car. The last glimpse I had of Farley's office, the bewildered young lieutenant was still sitting there in his shorts trying to figure out what the hell had come over the Army.

Just two hours from the time we'd crossed back into West Berlin, I was in an Army jet that was taking off as if the whole damned Russian air force were after it. I thought they were rushing things a little, but nobody was asking me.

It was one o'clock in the morning when the jet set down on the field in Washington. It had taken the bomber seven hours on the nose.

General Sam Roberts and a whole bevy of Army officers were already waiting at the field. They crowded around me and hustled me into a staff car. It took off as though it had just been shot out of a cannon.

I peered around in the car until I spotted the General. "What the hell's the rush?" I asked, digging him in the ribs with my elbow.

"All hell's almost loose," he growled. "You did a good job, boy—as I knew you would—but it's a little complicated."

"Like how?"

"Almost two hours ago, the Soviet authorities let loose a blast at us. Among other things, they mentioned sending you into East Germany as a spy and the matter of your assaulting two Russian officers and kidnapping two other men, one of them a citizen of East Germany."

"Now I get it," I said. "You're rushing to turn me over to the Russian Embassy."

He ignored me. "We have, of course, denied the whole story and have insisted that you have been back in the United States for several days. About an hour ago the reporters, including those from most of the foreign services, called and demanded to see you if you were in this country. We've stalled them, but right now they are all out in Hillyer's country home expecting you to step through the door any minute. You're going to."

About ten minutes later, we were out of Washington and the car turned into a driveway.

"This is the back way," General Roberts said. "We'll take you in the back door and then we'll go right into the press conference."

The car stopped beside the rear of a big colonial house and we all piled out and went in. Hillyer was there to meet us.

"You got here just in time," he said. "Hello, March. You did a great job."

"Thanks," I said.

"How long have the reporters been here?" General Roberts asked.

"About fifteen minutes."

"Good. What did you tell them?"

"That March was asleep and we were getting him up."

"Good," the General said again. He looked at me. "He looks as if he just got up, too." He reached out and straightened one of the oak leaves on my shoulder. "That goddam uniform doesn't fit you."

"Maybe you'd rather have had me show up in the Russian uniform I was wearing," I said.

"Don't even mention that word here. Let's go."

"There's just one thing," I said.

"What's that?"

"My discharge. I was supposed to have it the minute I landed. No discharge, no press conference."

"Don't be a goddam fool," General Roberts roared. "I can't give you a discharge here. You'll get it."

"Before I go out there," I said. "Maybe it ain't so formal, but you can just write it out on a sheet of paper. It'll stand up."

"Don't argue with him, do it," Hillyer said. He got a sheet of paper and the General scribbled on it, his face a dull purple. He handed it to me.

We went into the press conference.

General Roberts introduced me to the fifty or sixty newspapermen who were there. Then he made a little speech, denying the Soviet charge and offering me as evidence that they had trumped up the whole thing. Only nine and a half hours earlier I'd been driving that Cadillac in East Germany, so it made a pretty good story.

"Major March," one correspondent asked, "you were in Berlin, weren't you?"

"Almost a week ago," I said.

"For what purpose?"

"I went there to conduct an independent investigation of the defection of Hermann Gruss."

"Weren't you supposed to go into East Berlin and get Hermann Gruss?"

"That would be a pretty tall order," I said. "What paper did you say you were from? The *Tägliche Rundschau?*"

All the correspondents laughed.

"It's true," I went on, "that the East German press charged that's what I was there for, but that was the night before I left. I hate to disappoint the Kremlin, but I wasn't in East Berlin tonight."

"Where were you approximately nine hours ago, Major March?" one of the men asked.

I hadn't been rehearsed in that. "Well," I said, "I don't know if it's on the record or not, but General Roberts and I had a couple of dates. There's a twenty-dollar house over on—"

"The press conference is over," General Roberts roared. The newspapermen laughed, but they got up and started to file out.

"One of these days, March," General Roberts said slowly as the last one left, "do you know what's going to happen to you?"

"I know what's going to happen right now," I said. I took off my oak leaves and tossed them into his lap. "I'm going to bed and sleep. Lead me to a bed, Mr. Hillyer."

He did.

AFTERWORD

An Improbable Adventure?

"None of the characters is meant to portray any person living or dead." How often we read such a disclaimer at the beginning of a novel, as in the Author's Note for this one.

Several of the Milo March plots are based on real people or situations. *A Lonely Walk* (1956) has much in common with the still unsolved 1953 murder of a young Italian woman, Wilma Montesi. *The Gallows Garden* (1958) is a fictionalized account of the 1956 abduction and murder of a critic of the Dominican Republic dictator Rafael Trujillo. In *Wild Midnight Falls* (1968), Milo hunts down the twentieth century's most successful master spy, Richard Sorge. *The Bonded Dead* (1971) is based on a classic pattern of organized crime manipulating young Wall Street clerks into stealing bonds.

Ken Crossen estimated that about a fifth of the Milo March books were based on reality;* that would be four, an underestimation. But *The Splintered Man* may be the most unusual, in that it draws on two real-life situations, which the language of the Author's Note does not acknowledge.

At least two of the characters in *The Splintered Man* are

---

* Steve Lewis, "Interview with Kendell Foster Crossen," *The Mystery Nook,* no. 12 (June 1979), p. A3. This interview appears in the back of the Steeger Books edition of *No Grave for March.*

drawn from reality. Hermann Gruss is described as being "the head of the counterespionage police in West Germany. Before that he'd been a famous anti-Nazi, one of the few to escape after the unsuccessful bomb plot against Hitler." Now he'd gone over to Communist East Germany, in the company of a physician friend, Franz Oderbruch. Did Gruss defect voluntarily, or was he taken by force?

Consider the case of Otto John, who escaped the consequences of a failed bomb plot against Hitler in 1944 and who later became the first head of West Germany's domestic intelligence service. In 1954 John disappeared behind the Iron Curtain in the company of Dr. Wolfgang Wohlgemuth, a West German physician not unlike the fictional Dr. Oderbruch. Wohlgemuth had taken over the practice of Hitler's personal physician, a specialist in unorthodox drug therapies; Oderbruch is said to have taken over "the office and the practice of an important Nazi doctor who had been experimenting with drugs." (Wohlgemuth plied Hitler with opioids, methamphetamine, cocaine, and many other substances, but LSD was not on the list.) And both Oderbruch and Wohlgemuth are/were playboys.

Several days after he vanished, Otto John resurfaced in East Berlin, appearing to all the world like a defector. He subsequently went, or was taken, to the Soviet Union as well. In December 1955 he defected back to West Germany, where he was arrested. He now claimed that he had not moved willingly to East Berlin but was kidnapped by Communist agents after being drugged by Dr. Wohlgemuth (this might have been done with a pre-anesthetic sedative). The fictional

Gruss's situation is similar, although he claims that he went voluntarily with Dr. Oderbruch in order to receive medical treatment—which, we learn, the doctor deceived him into thinking he could only get in East Berlin. It is especially diabolical that the illness Dr. Oderbruch purported to cure was induced by him to begin with.

But wait—October 1955 is the publication date of *The Splintered Man,* two months before Otto John re-defected. So Crossen could not have known of John's revelations at the time he was writing a story somewhat consistent with them. Strange.

I would not have recognized the Gruss/John and Oderbruch/Wohlgemuth connections if I did not happen to have a letter written to Ken Crossen by his foreign rights agent in London, Elaine Greene: "I remember reading [*The Splintered Man*] with pleasure," she wrote on July 1, 1966, "and oddly enough, an Austrian friend who visited last week is engaged in helping Otto John with his memoirs which are due for publication fairly soon, which should make your book very timely again. I must say I used to like your idea of basing Chabers on actual happenings like John and Montesi." I am not alone in failing to recognize the Otto John connection; not one reviewer mentioned it, as far as I know. Did readers even know about John?

The second realistic issue that *The Splintered Man* raises is the sinister experimental use of drugs by a governmental agency (in this case, the East Germans), in which people were dosed with LSD without their knowledge or consent. Dr. Oderbruch is studying LSD for purposes of mind control, to make Gruss lose his will and reveal secrets that the U.S. had shared with him. Oderbruch is also said to be behind a special project to drug soldiers into total fearlessness for dangerous missions.

Originally published in 1955, *The Splintered Man* is the earliest fictional work to feature LSD, a fact that Ken Crossen was proud of. Robert Dickins, a scholar of the literature of psychedelic substances, told me, "As far as I know, it certainly was the first novel using LSD in its narrative— obviously I've not read everything that was published beforehand, but I've searched quite extensively and not found any earlier uses."*

Dickins comments on the novel in his master's thesis of 2012:

> ... toward the end it is revealed that the CIA also had the drug, and a Western agent [Henri Flambeau] who aids in the rescue describes it as having the ability to produce insanity in the user (Chaber 1955, 226). The implication is twofold: while Chaber may have been reassuring the reader that America was not lagging in its research, he was also alluding to the possibility the same experiments could be afoot in America. Whether or not the author knew it, the CIA had been testing the drug for some time.**

Whether or not he knew it? *Could* he have known it? In a later e-mail, Dickins cautiously termed it a guess: "For a

---

* E-mail to Kendra Crossen Burroughs, October 14, 2018.
** Robert John Dickins, "The Birth of Psychedelic Literature: Drug Writing and the Rise of LSD Therapy 1954–1964," thesis for the degree of Master of Philosophy in English, University of Exeter, 2012, pp. 46–48. The thesis can be accessed at http://psypressuk.com/2013/01/25/the-birth-of-psychedelic-literature-drug-writing-and-the-rise-of-lsd-therapy-1954-1964-by-robert-dickins/.

work of fiction, he was scar-
ily accurate in his guess that
the CIA were employing it for
mind-control purposes, and
many of their operations were
also in Berlin. He was either
very insightful or had some
inside information."*

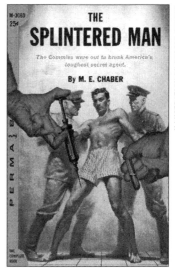

I can't imagine how Ken
Crossen would get inside
information about mind-control programs that tested
psychedelic and other drugs
on human subjects. However,
it's in the realm of possibility that *The Splintered Man,*
published in 1955, could have been based on such information. The secret program called MK-ULTRA was authorized
in 1953; its predecessors, code-named Artichoke and Blue-
bird, stemmed from1951 and 1950. These operations have
been called "the stuff of pulp fiction."**

I *can* imagine Ken reading the little square item that
appeared in the *New York Times* of November 29, 1953, under
the headline *Plunge Kills U.S. Defense Aide:* "A man identified as Frank Olson, a bacteriologist for the Defense Department in Washington, died early yesterday in a plunge from
a tenth-story [actually thirteenth-story] room of the Hotel

---

* E-mail to Kendra Crossen Burroughs, April 8, 2014.
** Introduction by Peter Levenda, in H.P. Albarelli, Jr., *A Terrible Mistake: The
Murder of Frank Olson and the CIA's Secret Cold War Experiments* (Trine Day,
2009), p. xiii.

Statler, Seventh Avenue and Thirty-third Street, the police reported. He was identified by Robert Vern Lashbrook, a Defense Department chemist. Mr. Lashbrook told the police that he had accompanied Mr. Olson here Nov. 24 and his friend had seen doctors about a depressed state...."

Crossen often said that Milo March was based on himself, and Milo has the habit of poring over newspapers; sometimes he finds a significant little article buried in the inside pages. A Defense Department employee plunging from a hotel room window might have caught the imagination of a pulp writer and spy novelist. I am not saying that Crossen knew what happened that day at the Hotel Statler, only that it is an interesting coincidence that Frank Olson, a bioweapons expert for the CIA, had been slipped a dose of LSD by a superior in the days before the tragedy, a fact the government did not admit until many years later.

I especially notice in the news clipping the sentence about Olson's seeing doctors for his depressed state. It was later revealed that he had complained of depression after being given the LSD, and the CIA sent him to a doctor (who was not even a psychiatrist). A variation on this scenario is the story of how Dr. Oderbruch, an amateur psychiatrist, pretends to treat Hermann Gruss for a nervous condition that the doctor himself engendered and then made even worse. Gruss was sent to a hospital and held there, while Olson agreed to go to a sanatorium but died before that could happen.

Frank Olson had something to be depressed about besides his unwanted LSD trip: in the year of his death, he had visited secret locations in Europe, where he witnessed "extreme interrogations in which the CIA committed murder using biological agents that Dr. Olson had developed," according to the Olson family's 2012 lawsuit against the U.S. government.* Not long afterward, he was taken to a CIA meeting where he unwittingly drank Cointreau laced with the insanity chemical. What must he have felt when it took effect? Did he think he was going mad, or did he know at once that he had been

poisoned? Were the hallucinations he endured as disturbing as the actual violence he had seen, and the torment of knowing that his research had made it possible?

How easily we accept the notion that an unanticipated LSD experience would drive a man to jump out a window. But that's not what Frank Olson did. After investigation, his two sons, Eric and Nils Olson, became convinced that their father had been drugged and thrown from the window—murdered by fellow agents because he knew too much. The story of his assassination and the government cover-up is told in the fictionalized Netflix documentary *Wormwood* (2017). This stranger-than-pulp-fiction murder mystery traumatized an

---

* "CIA sued over 1950s 'murder' of government scientist plied with LSD," http://www.theguardian.com/world/2012/nov/29/cia-lawsuit-scientist-1950s-death, accessed October 26, 2018.

entire family and, interestingly, led Frank Olson's nephew, Paul Vidich, to become a spy novelist.*

By comparison with true life, Milo's escapade doesn't seem so bad: faces taking on the long, droopy look of baboons, the carpet wriggling with red and yellow snakes; and Milo at least knows he is getting dosed. The Milo March adventures, despite some tough moments, are after all escapist reading, not horror stories.

I've learned that Whitey Bulger, the notorious organized crime boss, was also a victim of Mengele-like experimentation by the MK-ULTRA program—a coincidence, since Ken Crossen seems to have liked white-haired villains, two of whom are gangsters named Whitey in the Milo March series. Bulger gladly volunteered to participate while in prison in 1957, in exchange for a reduced sentence; he was also told that the research could help lead to a cure for schizophrenia. He set down in writing the effects LSD had on him, including blood oozing out of the walls, guys turning into skeletons, and his own head changing shape. "I felt like I was going insane," he wrote. Maybe he thought armed robbery was an everyday act of sanity (that was his worst crime at the time, as he had not yet been convicted of murder). Also coincidentally, in just days after I wrote these words, Whitey Bulger was murdered in prison, allegedly by a Mafia hit man.

I doubt Ken Crossen knew specifics about Frank Olson when he was writing *The Splintered Man,* because it was not until 1975, twenty years after the book's release, that the

---

* See https://crimereads.com/when-your-60-year-old-family-mystery-shows-up-on-netflix/.

public came to know about the covert program that killed Olson and made Bulger feel insane. MK-ULTRA was officially terminated in 1973, and LSD was abandoned as useless to the military. Allegedly. It's reasonable to assume that both the U.S. and Russia are still using drugs of many kinds in research into mind control and interrogation methods. In November 2018 it was revealed that the CIA had experimented with a truth-serum drug (a sedative called Versed) for use in interrogating terrorists after 9/11.*

LSD continued to interest Ken Crossen, or at least he still could still use it to sell stories. "The Twisted Trap," a short story in the pulp mode published in the men's magazine *Bluebook* in June 1961, features Milo March in his insurance investigator role. A wealthy old policyholder claims that his sexy young wife and her psychiatrist lover have teamed up to poison him with the drug and make him lose him mind. This is the title story of the final volume in the Steeger Books series, #23: *The Twisted Trap: Six Milo March Stories.*

Then there's *The Acid Nightmare,* a 1967 novel for teenagers that Ken said was written at the request of his publisher (Holt, Rinehart & Winston); it was reissued in 1972 in a Paperback Library edition. It tells the story of two acid trips taken by a young high school dropout. The first is groovy, full of music and colors. The second is the nightmare, because he is arrested and charged with a murder he doesn't remember committing while under the influence. *The Acid Nightmare* was one of Crossen's most successful books, probably due

---

* https://www.nytimes.com/aponline/2018/11/13/us/politics/ap-us-cia-interrogation-drugs-.html.

to school and library sales; adults must have felt it sent the right message to youth.

Of course, the characters in these works of fiction do not portray actual people or events. The *New York Herald Tribune Book Review* in 1955 had called *The Splintered Man* an "entirely improbable adventure" that M.E. Chaber made temporarily plausible. But this is how Ken Crossen concludes his statement that the characters are not intended to resemble real people: "Aside from that, any similarity to the world about us is entirely intentional."

Kendra Crossen Burroughs

Kendell Foster Crossen (1910–1981), the only child of Samuel Richard Crossen and Clo Foster Crossen, was born on a farm outside Albany in Athens County, Ohio—a village of some 550 souls in the year of this birth. His ancestors on his mother's side include the 19th-century songwriter Stephen Collins Foster ("Oh! Susanna"); William Allen, founder of Allentown, Pennsylvania; and Ebenezer Foster, one of the Minute Men who sprang to arms at the Lexington alarm in April 1775.

Ken went to Rio Grande College on a football scholarship but stayed only one year. "When I was fairly young, I developed the disgusting habit of reading," says Milo March, and it seems Ken Crossen, too, preferred self-education. He loved literature and poetry; favorite authors included Christopher Marlowe and Robert Service. He also enjoyed participant sports and was a semi-pro fighter in the heavyweight class. He became a practicing magician and had a passion for chess.

After college Ken wrote several one-act plays that were produced in a small Cleveland theater. He worked in steel mills and Fisher Body plants. Then he was employed as an insurance investigator, or "claims adjuster," in Cleveland. But he left the job and returned to the theater, now as a performer: a tumbling clown in the Tom Mix Circus; a comic and carnival barker for a tent show, and an actor in a medicine show.

In 1935, Ken hitchhiked to New York City with a typewriter under his arm, and found work with the WPA Writers' Project, covering cricket for the *New York City Guidebook*. In 1936, he was hired by the Munsey Publishing Company as associate editor of the popular *Detective Fiction Weekly*. The company asked him to come up with a character to compete with The Shadow, and thus was born a unique superhero of pulps, comic books, and radio—The Green Lama, an American mystic trained in Tibetan Buddhism.

Crossen sold his first story, "The Aaron Burr Murder Case," to *Detective Fiction Weekly* in September 1939, but says he didn't begin to make a living from writing till 1941. He tried his hand at publishing true crime magazines, comics, and a picture magazine, without great success, so he set out for Hollywood. From his typewriter flowed hundreds of stories, short novels for magazines, scripts radio, television, and film, nonfiction articles. He delved into science fiction in the 1950s, starting with "Restricted Clientele" (February 1951). His dystopian novels *Year of Consent* and *The Rest Must Die* also appeared in this decade.

In the course of his career Ken Crossen acquired six pseud-onyms: Richard Foster, Bennett Barlay, Kent Richards, Clay Richards, Christopher Monig, and M.E. Chaber. The variety was necessary because different publishers wanted to reserve specific bylines for their own publications. Ken based "M.E. Chaber" on the Hebrew word for "author," *mechaber.*

In the early '50s, as M.E. Chaber, Crossen began to write a series of full-length mystery/espionage novels featuring Milo March, an insurance investigator. The first, *Hangman's Harvest,* was published in 1952. In all, there are twenty-two Milo March novels. One, *The Man Inside,* was made into a British film starring Jack Palance.

Most of Ken's characters were private detectives, and Milo was the most popular. Paperback Library reissued twenty-five Crossen titles in 1970–1971, with covers by Robert McGin-nis. Twenty were Milo March novels, four featured an insur-ance investigator named Brian Brett, and one was about CIA agent Kim Locke.

Crossen excelled at producing well-plotted entertainment with fast-moving action. His research skills were a strong asset, back when research meant long hours searching library microfilms and poring over street maps and hotel floorplans. His imagination took him to many international hot spots, although he himself never traveled abroad. Like Milo March, he hated flying ("When you've seen one cloud, you've seen them all").

Ken Crossen was married four times. With his first wife he had three children (Stephen, Karen, Kendra) and with his second a son (David). He lived in New York, Florida, Southern California, Nevada, and other parts of the country. Milo March moves from Denver to New York City after five books of the series, with an apartment on Perry Street in Greenwich Village; that's where Ken lived, too. His and Milo's favorite watering hole was the Blue Mill Tavern, a short walk from the apartment.

Ken Crossen was a combination of many of the traits of his different male characters: tough, adventuresome, with a taste for gin and shapely women. But perhaps the best observation was made in an obituary written by sci-fi writer Avram Davidson, who described Ken as a fundamentally gentle person who had been buffeted by many winds.

Made in United States
Troutdale, OR
01/03/2025